PRAISE FOR *RIVERS*

Winner of the ECI Literature Prize 2016
Longlisted for the Fintro Literature Prize (Belgium)
Nominated for the Halewijn Prijs

"This is a book of controlled greatness, with sparklingly vivid sentences and an omnipresent threat, and at the same time it has a soothing timelessness."

—ECI jury chair Louise O. Fresco

"Writing well is not so hard, but sometimes a writer shows you what great writing is. The rivers here are not gentle: the waters are cruel and unpredictable. Water gives and takes. With Driessen, that which seems unchanging is unreliable. That is most prominent in the final story, where the dispute between two families on opposite sides of a Brittany stream a half a century ago is being fought with a persistence that makes the Israeli-Palestinian conflict seem like a café quarrel. Anti-Semitism plays a role in the background of all the stories, but so do sexuality, death, nature, and love. And above all, the river is a metaphor for Martin Michael Driessen's writing: fast-flowing, unpredictable, and at times stunningly beautiful."

—Arjen Fortuin, *NRC Handelsblad* (4 stars)

"Three remarkable story pearls. Driessen gives water a dramatic, almost apocalyptic meaning in the outstanding *Rivers*."

—*De Morgen*

"If there is justice in the world, then *Rivers* will bring Driessen the fame he deserves."

—*Haarlems Dagblad* (5 stars)

"Water continually plays the main role in this high-class book. Martin Michael Driessen is an original and unbridled storyteller. The best Driessen to date . . . Driessen's vivid narrative power achieves true perfection."

—*De Volkskrant* (4 stars)

"Staggering beauty."

—*Het Parool*

"It is rare, unfortunately, to read a story with every sentence perfect. But here, they are perfect."

—*Trouw*

"*Rivers* is the best thing I have read in years."

—*De Standaard* (5 stars)

"Each of the novellas feel much longer—like complete novels. *Pierre and Adèle*, my favorite, works so well because Driessen leaves a lot unsaid—a clear, epic story in supple, confident prose that leaves the reader space to dream. What more do you want?"

—*De Groene Amsterdammer*

"Three stories. Three times a world with a river as lifeline, as unbridgeable distance, as fodder for catharsis. Three times a small world mirrors the big one. Perhaps what they have most in common is the human desire to really reach one another. And all that in a language that grabs you with sentences you want to reread. The stories have a power you cannot escape from and language and images of great beauty."

—*Literair Nederland*

RIVERS

RIVERS

TRANSLATED BY JONATHAN REEDER

MARTIN
MICHAEL
DRIESSEN

This is a work of fiction. Names, characters, organizations, places, events, and incidents are either products of the author's imagination or are used fictitiously. Any resemblance to actual persons, living or dead, or actual events is purely coincidental.

Previously published as *Rivieren* in Holland by Uitgeverij G.A. van Oorschot B.V. in 2016. Translated from Dutch by Jonathan Reeder. First published in English by AmazonCrossing in 2018.

Published by AmazonCrossing, Seattle

www.apub.com

ISBN-13: 9781503901261 (hardcover)
ISBN-10: 1503901262 (hardcover)
ISBN-13: 9781503901278 (paperback)
ISBN-10: 1503901270 (paperback)

Cover design by Joan Wong

Printed in the United States of America

First edition

RIVERS

Fleuve Sauvage

All Comes to Naught

1

"If you have to drink, then do it someplace where it won't bother anyone," his wife had said.

"If you have to drink, then do it now," his agent had said. "Your Banquo rehearsals don't start until September."

"Sure, you can borrow my canoe and tent," his son had said, "but I'm not going out on that river with you. Is the point of this trip to drink yourself to death?"

It had rained nonstop the past few days, and the water level in Sainte-Menehould was uncommonly high for July. At dinner in Le Cheval Rouge, he drank wine; on his hotel bed, whiskey from the bottle he'd cracked open on the drive down from Brussels. He'd go alone, then. He knew that alcohol made him aggressive, and that others steered clear of him. In that regard, by now he had the forbearance of a leper. What held him back, he considered as he topped up the plastic bathroom cup with whiskey, was his rock-solid resolve. If he were to swear never to drink another drop, he would stick to it. Otherwise he would lose all self-respect, and it would be his downfall. He'd never be able to look himself in the mirror again if he broke a vow like that. So he had to weigh things up carefully before committing himself, because he'd be stuck with it for the rest of his life.

"You are an alcoholic," the doctor had said. "In your case, moderate drinking is not an option. You'll have to give it up altogether."

I'll think about that on the river, he thought. The bottle in my backpack might be the last one I'll ever drink. Say I make that decision. Marriage saved. Filial respect restored. Career at the National Theater stabilized. For ten years you'll look ten years younger, you might still have a shot at playing Hamlet. The bottle on the nightstand was nearly empty, but the one in his backpack was for the river. That, and a sedative and a half, should just about do it.

Do you really want to quit drinking? he thought as he lit a cigarette. It's not happiness, but it sure does feel like it. More than anything else you know.

2

The quay was flooded, and there was barely enough room to float under the first bridge. He pushed off. Sainte-Menehould was as sleepy as he was, this Sunday morning. The town was deserted. He paddled the canoe to the middle of the stream and crouched under the bridge's middle arch. When on the other side, he glided into the light and righted himself, and the rusty shutters of a house on the left bank opened. Three dark, wiry-haired girls appeared and waved excitedly. He waved back.

The canoe maneuvered well, only the bow stuck up too much, even though he'd stowed all the baggage up front. It was a long, aluminum one—too big, actually, for a man on his own. It had been a present for his son on his sixteenth birthday. That summer they traveled down the Loire together, a big chunk of it at least, past Chambord and the other famous château. That was after the promising first rehearsals for *Don Carlos*. Later, he'd lost his part for punching the assistant director, which even to this day he did not regret. A person without respect understands nothing of the theater.

Now the river flowed through overhanging trees and bushes, as it would for another few dozen kilometers, at least according to the prewar canoeing guide he had consulted the previous evening. *The Aisne*, he had read, *is an amiable river, which winds its way in countless meanders through the charming northern French countryside. Except for incidental tree blockages, one should encounter no major difficulties whatsoever until the large barrage at Autry*. All the better, he thought, I've got major difficulties enough.

It was still. The trees, with their balls of mistletoe, stood out against the pearl-gray morning sky. Muskrats splashed into the stream and dove underwater, as though startled by the appearance of the canoe. Swallows scattered from their nest-holes in the high, crumbling loam shores of the stream's outer banks in search of safety. *La France profonde*, he thought as he kept his course with gentle strokes. What more do you want?

After this morning's coffee, he couldn't imagine ever needing alcohol again. He couldn't even recall why he had needed it in the first place. He paddled around islands of lily pads, occasionally choosing to pass a gravel bank on either the left side or the right, but in fact the water did all the work. In the distance a church steeple came into view, but the name of the village didn't really interest him. It was getting warm; he took off his sweater. Another few kilometers and he'd stop for a rest. He would leave the whiskey in the backpack, but there was always that wine. The spot where he decided to pull ashore early that afternoon was an unfortunate choice: he sank up to his calves in mire and had to drag the canoe by its painter line through muck and cow dung. But he was suddenly tired and thirsty. It was a screw-cap bottle. The wine was lukewarm. He stretched out on the grass. He heard the rumble of traffic, and when he turned onto his side, he could see cars driving along a road at the foot of a row of hills. The spot was poorly chosen indeed, especially considering he had spent hours drifting through virtually pristine landscape. But he was thirsty, and put the bottle back to his lips. Just some supermarket Merlot, low alcohol, surely.

"Thou shalt get kings, though thou be none," he mumbled as he returned to the canoe half an hour later, and was sucked so deep into the mud that his sandals got stuck and he had to bend down to pull them out. Banquo was not a big role. He'd carry it off impressively, even if the young Polish director turned out to be an idiot. That they didn't dare cast him as Macbeth, he could understand. Even though that would have been the role of his life. He rinsed off the sandals, climbed into his canoe, and pushed off.

He was relieved to feel the current once again carry him along, around the next bend, into the shade of another patch of woods. The traffic noise soon died out. The slender Aisne flowed evenly and gracefully, bend by bend, under low-hanging branches that he occasionally parried with his paddle, like in an onstage swordfight. A kingfisher darted from shrub to shrub.

As the day wore on, he became drowsier and drank the rest of the Merlot as a pick-me-up. He felt that canoeing came easy to him; some things, like swimming, horseback riding, and love-making, you never forget. Even though he hadn't done these things in years. He did not stay midstream, but rather followed the current's swiftest course, which usually hugged the outside curves. He watched the sun: now to his left, now to his right, such were the river's wild meanders.

A fallen tree blocked his way. He tried back-paddling, but by then he was too close. The right bank, where the uprooted tree had once stood, was not an option, as the trunk lay too low above the water's surface to pass underneath it. The smashed crown rested on the opposite bank, but that still looked like his best chance.

"In the great hand of God I stand!" he shouted, gathering as much speed as he could and steering straight into the mass of branches and leaves. He got snagged, the canoe turned sideways at right angles to the current, an unexpectedly strong current, now that his upper half was stuck in the leaves; he leaned over, the canoe tipped to the larboard, and water gushed into the boat. He threw down the paddle, grasped at branches and twigs, and pulled himself with all his might deeper into the foliage.

"Damn'd be him that first cries: 'Hold, enough!'" he bellowed, although that wasn't one of Banquo's lines, but Macbeth's. Branches scraped his face, his anorak tore, and the front of the canoe was completely out of view, but he had regained control. The bow now pointed straight ahead again. He leaned forward and took hold of a large branch so as to pull himself farther downstream, but the canoe was still stuck. He stood halfway up and began rocking back and forth. Creaking and squeaking, the boat inched forward. When he felt he was nearly there, he sat back down. He made one, two more rocking motions, and the canoe broke loose and glided into the sunlight. He noticed blood on his hand, and wiped his face. A scar might well suit Banquo. He picked up the paddle and resumed his course. Torn-off leaves and twigs were strewn around his feet and the tarpaulin covering his gear.

The woods had passed, the Aisne now meandered through a landscape of open meadows, and an escort of exuberant heifers galloped along the high-lying banks with him. An unseen lark warbled jubilantly. The world seemed to him far more beautiful and rich on this side of the barrier than behind it.

Goddam, he thought. Goddam, my son couldn't have pulled this off.

3

After a couple of hours, he felt the need for a nip, but the one bottle was empty and the other was up at the front of the canoe. Unable to find a suitable place to stop, he put down the paddle and crept forward. The canoe wobbled, now floating sideways with the languid current, but he reached the bow without much effort.

When the day came to a close, he had no idea how many kilometers he had traveled. As the crow flies he was probably no more than ten kilometers from Sainte-Menehould, but no matter. He began scanning the banks for a suitable place to set up camp. A grassy patch above a low-lying riverbank, with no buildings in sight. It was dusk by the time he found what he was looking for.

He leaned the bottle of Merlot against the cooler—he'd lost the screw cap—and set up his tent. Stars appeared. That big one above the willows on the far side, that must be Venus. How far was it at most from the sun again? Forty-eight degrees, he seemed to remember.

The shadows of the night sped toward him from the east. France was quieter than ever. It was still warm, and he hung his damp towels, trousers, and socks over the branches of the huge willow under which he had left the canoe. Yet more stars came out. The creatures of the night were asserting their rights.

"I must become a borrower of the night for a dark hour or twain." He wondered which translation the hotshot Polish director would choose. If it turned out to be Claus or Komrij, he'd give them back the role. He wanted Burgersdijk. He knew the Banquo role inside out, at least in the original language.

He sat on the cooler; in it, the pâté and the salad he'd bought in Sainte-Menehould would have become suspiciously warm by now. He was not hungry. The tent flap was invitingly folded back, his sleeping bag unrolled, and his flashlight and cigarettes at hand. He was tired, but nothing more needed doing today. He drank and reflected. The night was now as dark as it would get at this time of year. Swallows—no, they were bats, surely—skimmed through the darkness. The Merlot was far from finished, but its vapid taste began to turn him off. As the screw cap was missing, he decided to hurl the bottle into the river. Whimsy was, after all, the best part about free will. That is what distinguishes us from animals, he mused. He simply felt like throwing the bottle into the river. He stood up and flung it, but heard no splash. Damn it, probably didn't throw it far enough, he thought, and walked down the riverbank to see where the bottle had landed, and also because he needed to piss.

"Freedom means being able to just chuck my beer cans into the woods," Hermann Scheidleder, a totally insane Austrian colleague, had once said. After he peed, without having found the bottle, he climbed back up the bank and got the Famous Grouse out of his backpack. The sharpness of the whiskey burned in his mouth, and he had the feeling of being cleansed, of once more becoming, for the moment, the person he really was. He swallowed, and the undisputable purity and strength of the alcohol filled him with deep satisfaction. Whoever does not know this feeling, he thought, doesn't know what they're missing.

That to-do with the assistant director had happened in Graz, during rehearsals for *Don Carlos*. He was Posa, because the director—who was it again, some stale old circus horse or other—had got it into his head that the marquis had to speak German with a Flemish accent. That had been his sole guest role abroad. Scheidleder was a flamboyantly mad Carlos, and everybody worshipped him during rehearsals, while he himself hardly got any notice at all, let alone recognition. In the canteen he had sought the support of the assistant director—who had, nota bene, studied dramaturgy—and suggested that his delivery of the line "Grant us liberty of thought, sire!" at that morning's run-through was really something quite unique.

She had cut her *knödel* into quarters and replied amiably: "Oh yes, compared to that, perfection is nothing."

Then he hit her. He was not sorry she had to be taken to the hospital, but did regret having let himself be provoked.

He held the whiskey bottle up against the moon. Still filled to just above the label.

Why don't I just sit here until I've figured out what I want to do with my life, he thought. Sleep can wait. It can't go on like this. I have to make choices.

Constellations he had earlier seen high in the heavens performed their somersault and fell downward to the dark tree line on the far side, like gymnasts having completed their jumps. Another three hours or so, and it would become light again. It was getting chilly. He took his sleeping bag from the tent, unzipped it, draped it over his shoulders, and sat back down on the cooler.

If I keep this up, I know how it will go and how it will end.

"If you don't stop drinking now," his doctor had said, "it will be too late. You're on the verge of cirrhosis. It's now or never."

"The only good thing about cirrhosis," he had said to his worried impresario, "is that I don't have to talk to you about it."

If I were to quit drinking today, everything will be different. Do I want that? Do I want things to be different? Even his wife, Minou, had landed in the hospital on occasion, but she had never pressed charges.

Say I decide here and now to swear off booze for good. Let's say when this bottle of Famous Grouse is empty. That would mean that on the very first day of this trip, I've made a decision I've got four more days to make. It'll take at least that long to reach Vouziers. And besides, I've been drinking, so how do I know if I am in my right mind when I make this decision? It's like looking through blue glasses. What an idiotic expression. But I've still got time to think it over.

But he could no longer ignore what he knew deep down: it was indeed now or never. This was the first time in years he'd spent the night under the open sky. Within sight of the canoe he had bought for his son, and in which, in happier times, they had paddled down the Loire together.

It's now or never, he thought. Now or never. Damn it all, why can't saintliness be deferred? If I get up right now and throw this nearly full bottle into the Aisne, I'll be losing a hell of a lot. And forever, mind you, because there's no turning back. I owe that to myself. I'll have to pick up where I left off at age eighteen. As though I haven't lived. As though everything up till now has been worthless.

He stood up. I'm going to do it, he thought, and shuddered. Wrestling with the angel is wrestling with yourself. And one of us will lose. But I'm going to do it, then there's no turning back. I won't even take one last swig. He climbed to the highest point of the bank, braced himself, and flung the whiskey bottle into the middle of the river. This time there was a massive splash, a nocturnal bird flew up and screeched, and he felt like the knight who had thrown the sword Excalibur into the water.

He pulled the canoe further up the bank, just to be sure, because it appeared that the river had swollen. He dragged the sleeping bag behind him into the tent and zipped the flap shut.

4

The following morning he made Nescafé on the portable camp stove, and shaved in a small mirror he had hung on a branch with a piece of wire. There were heavy bags under his eyes, and as he had no blow-dryer, his hair was draped over his head like soggy palm fronds. So this is how a man looks who no longer drinks, he thought. When you were young, you thought your mug would be at its best after forty, but now you're pushing sixty, and you haven't made a whole lot of progress. "Damned actors!" the old director in Graz used to remark. He was regularly quoted in the theater's canteen: "First they booze it up until their noggin's finally got a bit of character, and then they can't remember any of their lines."

It must have rained heavily upstream, for the river had risen even more. Low-lying meadows had turned into lakes.

The Aisne continued to wind through open land, and according to his guide, there wouldn't be any more wooded banks before the weir at Autry.

This high water made canoeing easy; he could pass tree obstacles either to the left or the right. A swan took off when he approached, and then swept forward past him, just above the water's surface. It was overcast and less warm than yesterday. No longer used to physical exertion, he raised and lowered his shoulders every so often to relieve his muscles. After the next bend in the river, he spotted the swan again, about a hundred meters up ahead. And so the game continued: as soon as he approached, the swan would take off and swoop past him downstream. *"Mein lieber Schwan,"* he tried to sing, but he could only remember a few notes from *Lohengrin*, and no more lyrics than these.

He had covered, he thought, quite some river kilometers without taking a single break. If the river keeps on swelling and the water keeps rising, he thought as the banks raced past him with the speed of a cyclist, I'll be in Vouziers before I know it. As afternoon approached, he noticed the same swan accompanying him again, as though acting as an escort; each time the canoe drew near, it flew a few hundred meters further, landing with outstretched wings. Then it drifted for a while in the middle of the river, seemingly uninterested in anything else, until he nearly caught up with it. It did not do as most other waterbirds did—timidly taking cover at the riverside and then, once you've almost passed them, fleeing panic-stricken in the opposite direction. But it did not do what you might expect from an ostensibly superior animal like the swan: take off, circle halfway, and land far behind the intruder. Again and again it swam out ahead of the canoe, a bit concerned, it seemed, then took off and waited for him a ways further downstream.

"Du blö-der Schwan," he sang, "you stupid swan," improvising to his four-note *Lohengrin* motive. He paddled more energetically than really necessary: he felt strong, as if he were already beginning to feel the effect of his total abstinence.

When the sun eventually touched the tops of the willows, he realized he hadn't a drop of alcohol on board. But that was irrelevant. He had, after all, decided never again to touch another drop. Over and done with. At a certain point, the swan, too, was gone. Night was falling, but he paddled on, partly because he did not know what to do with the rest of his evening once he'd set up his tent. And this was magical, floating into the darkness. It was almost noiseless now. All he heard were the sounds of the wide, flowing river, the call of an owl. The cows that he could still make out on the riverbank stood or lay chewing their cud, and they showed, for their part, scant interest in a man in a canoe. The stars elbowed their way above the black silhouette of the treetops. And he moved on effortlessly, meeting no further obstacles.

I've never set up a tent in the dark, he thought, but luckily I've got that lamp to strap to my forehead, like the eye of a cyclops.

It would be just the ticket in a confrontation, should anyone harass him. He would blind his assailant while keeping his own hands free. He had vast experience in dispensing with troublemakers. To the police officers who tried to make him sign a drunk driving report after he got behind the wheel of his Jaguar thoroughly inebriated, following the premiere of *The Caucasian Chalk Circle*, he had said, "If you claim that I am too drunk to drive a car, how then do you expect me, in my condition, to sign a statement?"

And then that forest ranger. He was walking in the woods somewhere in Brabant; his dog was unleashed and chasing deer, and the man asked, "You are a nature lover, aren't you, sir?"

He had countered with, "Do you know what a rhetorical question is?"

That was superb; this riposte belonged to his opening repertoire ever since, and as far as he was concerned, it was as classic as the Sicilian or King's Indian in chess. Equally brilliant was his next move, when he had allowed the case to come to court and explained why he refused to sign that police report: "Your Honor, I do not wear reading glasses in the wilds."

And his endgame was likewise masterly, when the judge imposed a fine of two thousand francs.

"Stupidity has its price," he had said.

"I'm glad you realize that," the judge responded.

To which he benignly replied, "I didn't mean mine, Your Honor."

By now he had a great variety of retorts up his sleeve, should anyone bedevil him, under any circumstances, and he rehearsed them as regularly as a chess master does his theory.

He did not consider himself at all pugnacious, but it was best not to cross him.

He went ashore at a sort of mud-banked peninsula enclosed in barbed wire on iron staves, presumably placed to keep the cows from straying at low water. By now it was pitch-dark, too late to be choosy, so he headed for the spot where the barbed wire was lowest; the aluminum hull scraped over it with an awful screech, and to keep his sandals clean, he took them off before stepping into the mire, holding his canoe by the painter. The bank was high, not hopelessly steep but enough so that he thought, What the hell, the boat can stay in the water tonight. Before tying it up he collected the most essential gear—tent, sleeping bag, mat. It started to rain. Time to call it a day.

As he fastened the canoe to one of the iron staves, a bottle drifted past. He bent over, scooped it out of the water, and held it up.

Famous Grouse. The bottle he had thrown into the river had caught up with him.

5

He managed to get the tent set up in the pouring rain, although he was unable to keep his things from getting wet until they could be stowed under the fly. He had attached just three guy-lines instead of the sixteen that, along with the stakes, were in the oblong bag, and he'd tripped over those three lines repeatedly before he could take refuge inside the tent with just the essentials. This meant leaving the rest of his gear down below, and that the canoe would fill with rainwater during the night, but there was nothing to be done. He did not have the strength to go back down again, empty out the canoe, and flip it over.

This is back to basics, he told himself. This is what life in the great outdoors is all about. He would manage to sit out the rest of this short summer night with what little he had at hand. He undressed and stuffed his wet things in a corner of the fore-tent. Without giving it any further thought, he put the whiskey bottle to his mouth and drank. A gift from the river gods, he thought. It was meant to be. Wisdom is knowing when not to think. He felt more contented than he had in ages, lying there in his clammy sleeping bag, listening to the rain, and every so often, putting the bottle to his lips.

He had almost dozed off when he heard the sounds. Heavy footsteps. Panting and snorting. The tent fabric above his head was being pressed in. Cows. Now all he needed was for them to get snagged on the guylines, fly into a panic, and trample the tent. He strapped the lamp to his forehead, unzipped the sleeping bag, buckled on his sandals, and climbed outside.

There were a good twenty of them. They stood in a semicircle around the tent in the starlight, and at the sight of him, they retreated slowly, their heads hanging low. The boldest and most inquisitive promptly took a step forward.

"Go away, you!" he shouted, and walked toward them, waving his arms. They withdrew hastily, like a regiment in panic, and when he took a few more brisk steps in their direction, the battle line broke; they turned and scattered in all directions, colliding with one another, and trotted and galloped off, chaotic and ridiculous.

"Go away!" he yelled again.

They came to a halt a safe distance away and looked back at him. He saw the silhouettes of twenty-some pairs of ears against the firmament.

"Leave me be," he warned as he climbed back into his tent. He removed his wet sandals and dried himself off, took a swig of whiskey, and inspected the bottle in the light of his headlamp. There wasn't much left, but it was enough to put him to sleep.

When he settled down and switched off his lamp, it started anew. The heavy footsteps, the snorting. It sounded more agitated and wary than before. Maybe they'll go away on their own, he thought. But after ten minutes this was not the case. He heard something scrape against the tent fabric and switched the lamp back on.

The bright beam revealed a large black tongue rasping against the thin nylon. Furious, he put on his sandals and bolted out of the tent. They really had to leave him in peace, these animals. He gathered branches and stones and began pelting the herd, which had retreated a bit when he emerged. They sluggishly turned their heads toward where his projectiles landed. Even when he did hit one of them, it had little effect on the others. They were like aliens who did not understand why they were not welcome on Earth.

It's impossible to sow panic among an enemy this stupid, he thought. No field marshal would be a match for them. One animal in particular, almost solid white but with a black head, proved unflappable, and after every sortie took another inquisitive step closer. Goddammit, he thought, I'll light a torch. That'll teach you.

Just then a car approached. The headlight beams lengthened and shortened, in keeping with the contours of the rough terrain. He had just enough time to pull on his jogging pants, because apart from his sandals he was naked, before confronting the blinding double sun of the headlights and the two sun dogs that detached themselves on either side, in the form of powerful flashlights, with a truculent "You are the owner, monsieur?"

"Oui," came the answer from behind the barrage of light. "What are you doing here?"

He explained that he was only camping. The voice, which sounded very peculiar, as though it belonged to someone who had had throat cancer and now relied on an electronic speech apparatus, said that he should have asked for permission in advance and that he had to leave immediately. He said that this was not realistic, but that he would be gone in a couple of hours. The *propriétaire* said he would notify the gendarmerie.

He thanked him for his hospitality and said he would be gone before dawn, without leaving behind so much as a trace of his sojourn. Eventually the sun dogs melted back into the double sun of the headlights, and doors slammed shut. He caught a glimpse of the second person, who only got in once the car had turned to leave. It was a young woman, still a girl, in a dark skirt and gumboots. As the car withdrew he could see the cows following the red taillights in an elongated caravan, most likely in the direction of the farm.

He was relieved, his adrenaline dropped, he nipped from what was still in the bottle.

But an hour or so later, just as he was about to fall asleep, it started again. The snorting. The licking of the tent roof. Livid, he crawled back out into the rain, this time barefoot, determined to put an end to it once and for all. Someone had once explained to him that a problem with livestock farming was that herds are not naturally structured. Normally you'd have a bull, cows of various ages, and calves. But if you put a whole slew of young animals of the same age and sex together, like yearlings and heifers, you're asking for trouble. It becomes a gang of juvenile delinquents. An ensemble should consist of all age groups, too, not only young Romeos, like in his company.

By the time he had pulled the cyclops lamp onto his head and switched it on, he found himself face-to-face with the white heifer with the black head. They were intolerably large and profound female eyes—the last thing he was in the mood for right now. Each ear sported a yellow clip with the number 234. The animal stood, legs apart, in front of the tent and gazed at him. He scrambled upright, cursing. The heifer lifted her tail and spewed shit over his cooler.

He took three quick steps forward, and with all his might smacked her head with the whiskey bottle. It made a heavy thump, like a sledgehammer striking an anvil. The bottle did not break. The cow took a few steps back, the horns low, as if preparing for a counterattack. He heard the rest of the herd beat a retreat. But the white heifer with the black head stayed put, as though determined to do anything to salvage their relationship. He ran at her, the bottle raised. Eventually she made a clumsy sort of pirouette and attempted to flee. He did not know what possessed him, but he cut her off and forced her onto the neck of land above where his canoe was moored. The animal was cornered.

"Avaunt, and quit my sight! Let the earth hide thee!" he bellowed and swung the bottle again.

She dodged skittishly to one side and lost her balance. Her hind leg slipped over the edge of riverbank, and for a moment he saw half a cow. That, too, disappeared from view, and he heard the animal, panting and gargling, roll down the steep bank. There was a dull thud, like a heavy projectile hitting sludge, and immediately thereafter the plaintive lowing began. He went over to the edge. The heifer lay next to his canoe. One foreleg was outstretched in an unpromising position, and the other was buckled underneath the body. The hind legs, conversely, lay serenely alongside one another. But one of the iron staves to which the barbed wire was attached stuck out of her flank. The beast had impaled itself.

Goddammit, he thought, what now? The heifer bellowed nonstop between rasping breaths. It wouldn't be long before the farmer heard it. He had no idea how to put an animal this size out of its misery. Chalk it up to experience, he thought. Never commit a crime while canoeing down a river. You've been spotted, and you can't run.

For the second time, he flung the cursed bottle, which was not yet completely empty, into the Aisne, and returned to his tent. Get dressed, he thought. Money, papers, car keys. You never know what will happen next, but you have to be prepared. As he was doing this, the green nylon roof of his tent lit up. Car headlights. How much would a heifer like that be worth? He would pay, if necessary. On an impulse he tucked his Opinel pocketknife into his pants pocket.

The floodlights glided off the tent, a car door opened and shut, and while he hastily tied the laces of his hiking boots, he heard a girl's voice scream: "Oh, *non*. Non, non. Non! Tétine!"

So number 234 had a name too.

She thrashed at the tent with such a fury that it nearly collapsed. If there had been a door, she'd have kicked it in.

He unzipped the fly and stuck out his head. Before him stood the same girl as before, the one with the dark skirt and the gumboots.

"The earth hath bubbles, as the water has," he mumbled sardonically. This is what Banquo says after having seen the witches.

"Quoi?" she shrieked, and pointed to the river. "Come and help me!"

She ran to the bank, sat down, and slid over the edge. The unseen heifer wailed unrelentingly. He climbed down the steep bank. She was crouched alongside the animal, one hand clamped on the iron stave that had pierced its flank.

"Oh, *ma pauvre* Tétine . . . wait, wait."

When he reached her, she looked up. A nondescript, lanky farm girl. A Joan of Arc type, only not pretty enough. She stood up surprisingly fast.

"What have you done?" she bawled. "You'll pay for this. My father has already called the gendarmerie. Bastard! Help me!"

He tried to help. They attempted to pull out the rod upward, but the animal lay on top of the barbed wire attached to it.

"We have to roll her over . . . cut the barbed wire . . . quick!" They bundled their strength in an effort to get Tétine rolled onto her other flank, she tugging on the forelegs and he on the far heavier hindquarters. He felt like a hero in one of those action films, where an older but strong and experienced man comes to the aid of a young woman, for instance if they became stranded on a desert island. That was his kind of movie. He leaned back with his full weight, the cow's surprisingly thin ankles in his fists, but there was no budging her. Maybe the barbed wire had dug deep into her flesh. The girl stood with her gumbooted feet in the mud, legs apart. Her woolen cap had glided off her head.

"Fair is foul, and foul is fair," he panted, and suggested that it might be best to put the animal out of its misery. He removed the Opinel from his pocket and showed it to her.

When they let go of her legs, Tétine gargled and dragged her head sideways through the mud, as though trying to distance herself from the pain in her hindquarters.

"Shut up, you lush!" she shrieked, and slapped him in the face.

He dropped the knife, and before he knew it, he had grabbed her by the neck. This was unacceptable. She had hit him. She had no respect. She fell onto her back, half leaning up against the cow's belly. He straddled her body and squeezed her throat. His knees sank deep into the lukewarm mire.

I might not know how to slaughter a cow, but this, this I know, flashed through his mind.

Her hands, at first vainly gripping his wrists, fell back into the sludge. After a couple of minutes, he struggled upright.

Goddammit, he thought. The cow was still bellowing, without any inkling of the gravity of the situation. He looked around him, he looked up at the stars, but did not see anything out of the ordinary. She suddenly moved and stared at him with wide-open eyes. It was very bad, what was happening here. It was wrong. All he wanted was for it to be over. He grabbed her by the ankles and pulled her off the cow. He dragged her half into the river, took her head, turned it, and pushed it underwater, without paying any heed to the rest of her body or to who she was. Suddenly, rain started coming down in buckets again. The heavy raindrops formed bubbles on the surface of the water, which drifted downstream like miniature domes. He got up and wiped the hair from his forehead. Her skirt, sopping wet, was hitched up to her hips. Her skinny legs were not pretty, round and white as flagpoles. Her boots lay flat in the mud, like the wilted stems of some plant or other. He tried to clamber up the slippery bank, but kept sliding back down. What a terrible spot he'd chosen to set up camp. He'd have to be more careful in the future. He did manage to get a bit further along.

He went over to the parked car, its engine still running and headlights lit, and removed the key from the ignition. He switched off the lamp on his forehead. The world was dark, the rain persisted, and there wasn't a star to be seen.

"There's husbandry in heaven," Banquo says in the second act, "their candles are all out." He had to leave at once and cover his tracks. He tripped on a guyline and thought, I haven't had too much to drink, have I? No time to roll up his sleeping bag and mat. He yanked the tent out of the ground, pegs and all, and threw the shapeless bundle over the edge. The rest of his gear followed. He slid down the bank, covered from head to toe in mud like a golem, and began tossing everything into the canoe.

The farmer with the electronic voice, presumably the girl's father, had seen him. His name and domicile were on the register of Le Cheval Rouge in Sainte-Menehould. He threw her car keys into the river. He wasn't a thief, nor had he raped her.

"Your Honor," he would address the court, "the prosecution is overlooking one crucial detail." He suddenly panicked, unable to locate his paddle. He wouldn't have put it somewhere too low, would he, so that it . . . but there it was, at the bottom of the canoe. "He maintains that killing a young girl, with her whole life before her, is a particularly heinous crime, and in that sense more reprehensible than murdering a man or an adult woman. But as Schopenhauer said: 'With girls, Nature has in view what is called in a dramatic sense a "striking effect." Girls are prized and idolized, loved and lauded, admired and desired, more than any other human being.' And I therefore ask you . . ."

He could not get the cooler, which always fit squarely under the middle thwart, into place. "I therefore ask you, Is it not obviously a case of natural logic that this specific form of attention is more likely to fall upon young girls than other people, by which I mean to say, that they are murdered more often?"

He assumed he hadn't forgotten anything. There was nothing else lying around. The rain pattered steadily. Water had collected in the bilge to above the floor slats, which would make the canoe unstable. But everything was loaded; it was too late to flip it over. The heifer no longer moved. Her head lay half submerged, an alligator with horns. The water around her hindquarters appeared dark. The girl's upper body was also underwater, as if she were searching for her car keys.

Can't help you there anymore, he thought. "Is there perhaps some sort of atavistic jealousy behind the prosecutor's call for the maximum sentence?" The willows across the river became white, like an overlit theater set: car headlights. He untied the canoe, climbed in, and pushed off. The current carried him along as though nothing had ever happened. Faster and faster he glided past the dark rows of trees. The river, now vastly wider, was unrecognizable compared to two days ago. This was a rain-swelled Amazon pushing its way through nocturnal northern France. But he felt equal to the task; he navigated with a sure hand through bends that he felt more than saw. As an experiment he switched on his headlamp, but then he saw only the gleaming aluminum bow and nothing of the river. Better to travel in the dark. The patter of the rain and the gurgling of the river were joined by another continually swelling sound: dull, like breaking surf, but without its somber rhythm. It was as if the polyphonic song of the water transporting him gradually modulated toward an irrevocable closing chord.

Before him, everything was black. A dam, a barrage, a weir, the edge of the world, the end of the world as he knew it. Maybe the end of the world was made of concrete. But something else loomed ahead: a high, black cliff and at its foot, white surf. The current gathered speed, and he knew there was nothing to be done. He held his paddle crosswise. The bow plunged into a mass of foam, there was a thud, the boat twisted as though steered by the hand of spirits, and capsized. The river was not cold, and underwater it was quiet.

This is my end, he thought, but I needn't be ashamed because no one can see me. I am alone here. Forever alone, even more than on stage. He surfaced no further than his eyes, he made no effort to breathe. He was finished. He spread his arms and felt the current pin him against a fallen tree. The curve of the trunk pressed his head down against his chest. He screamed against his will, and the river surged, roaring into his mouth. And all of a sudden, everything went silent.

Remember this, he thought, because this is the last thing you will know, soon you will be dead.

He saw Minou approach him, her arms spread wide, like the first time, when they both passed their entrance exam for the theater school.

Life was good, he thought, only I'd like to have played Macbeth.

6

The next morning, at the bend in the river near Ivoy Farm, all they found was the farmer's Toyota minus the ignition key. The flooded river had washed away the bank where the stranger had camped.

Several hours later the gendarmes made their discovery, a hundred meters upstream from the Autry barrage parking lot.

Sloshing against the trunk of a tree that had fallen across the river was a filthy carpet of debris made up of rotting reeds, foliage, plastic buckets, and all manner of refuse the river had dragged with it. And in that permanent wash of garbage, affixed to the tree trunk by the ferocity of the current that had reached its highest levels since 1972, they saw a capsized aluminum canoe, the shapeless remains of a wadded-up tent, the bloated cadaver of a heifer, a cooler, and the body of a young woman lying on the chest of a dead man, an empty bottle clutched in his hand.

Voyage to The Moon

Life Is a Dream

Durlacher's house was the only one in the village with an upstairs. They had gotten up in the middle of the night and waited until a lamp was lit behind the windows.

It was the first time fourteen-year-old Konrad was allowed to join them to float the tree trunks. The coat he was wearing had belonged to his older brother, who had drowned last summer. His mother had hemmed up the sleeves. The half-moon was darkened by clouds pushing eastward.

The light went on.

"About time," old Schramm muttered.

"Now Mother'll have to make coffee first," Hinzpeter said peevishly and spat out a squirt of chewing tobacco.

A quarter of an hour later, Durlacher came out, followed by his son Julius.

He wore a long loden coat and a hat; Julius had on a loden pea jacket with little antlers embroidered on the collar, and a large round cap of soft gray felt.

"Looks like the lad's put a tea cozy on his head," Hinzpeter whispered.

"Morning, men," Durlacher said.

"Morning, sir," they replied.

It was a three-hour walk to the log stacks at the creek. They took the shortest route to the forest. The small, shabby houses at the foot of the hill were for the day laborers, widows, and men who were too old or too infirm to work as floaters or lumberjacks. At home, the shutters were still closed; Konrad's mother was still asleep. A hundred meters up, the road became a wooded path.

Durlacher and his son, holding lanterns, walked in front. They each carried a peavey, the long pike with the wrought hook needed for this work. Konrad carried his brother's.

At 7:20, the weirmaster would open the sluice, and then the creek would briefly convey enough water to drive the loose tree trunks down to the sawmills. Durlacher had contracts with the mills. If anything went wrong, he'd have to wait until the reservoir filled up again, which could take weeks. So only the best men in the village were eligible to drive the logs, and Konrad was proud that he was now one of them.

He had to take large strides to keep up with old Schramm, Hinzpeter, and the silent giant Ekkehart, who was the strongest man in the village but had two left feet, so he seldom went on a raft.

To be one of the rafters was Konrad's dream. The spar rafts were made of the sturdiest, longest tree trunks, and every year they were floated, lashed into ever-larger strings, down the Rodach, the Main, and the Rhine, until they reached Holland.

This was the beginning: short trunks—three meters at most—were driven down the temporarily flooded creek to the mills in the valley, where they would be sawed into planks. That was the first step. If Durlacher approved, maybe next year he would be allowed to ride with them on a raft, into the wider world.

The first leg of the climb was steep, but living in the mountains, one got used to the slow pace of things. Every uphill road is a slow one. Drizzle changed to wet snow. Konrad trod in Ekkehart's footsteps. He panted and did not look up or around, for he needed all his attention to keep from falling behind. The light from the oil lamps shone on bramble bushes, tree trunks, and glistening boulders, but the path they followed was almost entirely dark.

It became light. The crowns of tall pines jutted through the mist into the pale morning sky, like inquisitors who held his fate in their hands. Konrad thought the woods were ugly. The branches sagged under the drizzle and dew, and clouds hung in dales and crevices like dull-gray worms. It was dead quiet except for that dripping and the thud of a falling pine cone. Everything smelled of sap and damp decay. Birds and other animals made themselves scarce.

But he looked forward to driving the timber that had waited under the snow all winter and would now, finally, embark on a journey.

They arrived at the creek. From this point they would follow the bed. Durlacher blew out the lanterns. They proceeded in single file, shouldering their long peaveys like pikemen on their way to ambush an unwary enemy.

The gully was dry. A stripe separating the boulders in light and dark halves showed how high the water had stood last year. The stripe resembled the one on the hemmed sleeves of Konrad's coat.

The dry creek bed was filled with logs, a moraine of wood. More trunks were stacked parallel to the creek. Durlacher unbuttoned his loden coat and checked his pocket watch.

"Seven-twenty, men," he said. "Get ready."

The men were ready. The controlled flood would last fifteen minutes, at most.

A few minutes later a primordial rumble sounded in the haze above them, and then a white plow of water came crashing down the hill, shifted the trunks, lifted them up, and carried them away. Konrad leapt forward and, using his pike as a lever, rolled the next trunk into the creek, following it with his eyes—how it dipped and rocked as it floated downstream, twisted sideways, rammed into the rocks, and then got brought back on course. This was the first trunk he'd ever driven. This was the beginning of his life as a man.

"Stay back, Julius!" Durlacher bellowed. "Keep away from there! What'll I do if you break a leg? Just watch how it's done, I told you."

Konrad watched with amazement how weightless the trunks became once they entered the water.

Where brawn and leverage had to do the initial work, they now, as though in a fairy tale, glided effortlessly downstream with the glistening water. A swarm of spears. Never before had he seen anything so beautiful.

Julius attended the academic gymnasium in Kronach; Konrad worked as a journeyman. They only saw each other when Julius stood on the shore, watching the logs being driven. His father felt he should have practical experience; all well and good, that "Gallia est omnis divisa in partes tres," *but after all, Julius was his heir and would eventually have to run the business. Julius was ever the model* gymnasiast, *always dressed to the nines, typically in gray loden, with a soft cap covering his ash-blond hair. Konrad couldn't care less about Latin; he longed for life on the big rivers.*

But for now this was denied him. Durlacher did not hire him for the real job, that annual event where the women and girls assembled on the bridge and along the quay to admire the steersmanship of the full-fledged raftsmen, who stood tall, legs apart, and steered the wooden capital downstream, deftly pushing off against bank and riverbed in their oiled hip waders, their pride and joy.

Konrad yearned to be one of those men. He wanted to join them on those immense floating islands that sailed down the Rhine, bigger than any ship, for they were strung together in such a way that they could follow the meanders of the river like huge, prehistoric wooden snakes. He wanted to see the wealthy Dutch cities, which in fact were built upon their very own woods, because those proud stepped and curved gables and brick towers rested upon a subterranean forest of Franconian trees.

But Durlacher would not let him.

Only when Julius had reached his final year of gymnasium, as *Oberprimaner*, did he and Konrad first strike up a conversation.

The men had once again assembled outside Durlacher's house in the middle of the night and waited for a light to go on. Schramm was there, Hinzpeter and the Halder brothers too. It had thawed, and there was a good chance that this year they would have no problem driving all the logs, as the reservoirs were filled to the rim, and meltwater already flowed in part of the bed.

Konrad and Julius walked side by side behind Durlacher and his men. The pines dripped, water droplets beaded on their loden coats and pea jackets. Julius shifted his peavey over his head to his left shoulder so they could walk closer together.

After proceeding like this for some time in silence, he whispered, "Say, when I take over the firm I'll see to it that you get to be a rafter."

Durlacher stopped, as he did every year, at the large boulders.

"Father—may I join Konrad this time?" Julius asked.

"I'd rather you stay here with me," Durlacher replied.

"You want me to learn the trade, don't you? Then I'll have to have done everything once myself. I've already seen how they roll the logs often enough. Let me have a go, with Konrad."

The other men had already begun the steep climb up the bed, striding ahead without so much as a sideways glance.

Durlacher thought it over. "As you like. But watch yourself."

They each took one side of the bank and leaned on their pikes. The bed was not very wide; they stood at most five meters apart. The mist lifted, the sky went white, a pair of crows whizzed above their heads in a screeching dispute that apparently needed to be resolved further up.

"When the logs come down," Konrad warned, "stand back and watch me first, d'you understand? Only try it yourself once you've seen how it's done."

"Righty-ho!" Julius called back.

The first trunks came at them almost with the very first rush of water, side-by-side, like rival boats in a regatta, and Konrad did nothing except to give them the occasional nudge with his peavey to lead them past the boulders; in fact, even this was hardly necessary, as they showed no sign of wanting to twist sideways as they dipped down the gorge.

"You see?" he called. "Just guide them—let the water do the work."

Julius aimed the point of his peavey at a crooked, furiously rolling trunk. He missed and nearly tumbled headfirst into the water.

"Be careful, man!" Konrad shouted.

He guided the logs with the routine of a farmer driving his livestock through a gate; he did no more than necessary, aside from a push here and a tug there just to keep a feel for the current.

Julius, on the other hand, regarded every trunk that came by as a personal challenge, whether it needed his help negotiating the gully or not. He tried too hard and wore himself out without actually doing anything useful.

Half the logs had already passed. Konrad was engrossed in the gurgling of the creek and the stately procession of the felled trees on their way to the sawmills.

Suddenly, far longer trunks, too long to pass through the gully, appeared. They couldn't be Durlacher's, because he always cut his to a specified length.

"Back off!" Konrad shouted. "Watch out!"

The first oversized trunk forced its way head-on into the gap in the rocks, but the current dragged it askew, and it became jammed across the creek. The trunks that followed rammed the newly formed barrier, creating a stationary raft unable to move in any direction. The bed became clogged with logs, and water gushed over and around them. The long trunks kept on coming, like pirate ships cornering an unsuspecting fleet of merchant ships, until they had formed a crosswise wall of logs, blocking the gorge.

Konrad had never experienced anything like this before.

"The bottom one has to be pried loose!" Julius shouted, and waded into the creek, his pike poised for action. He underestimated the force of the water. Of course there was no getting the tangle of timber to budge; one would have to wait for the reservoir to run dry before unraveling this mess, which meant hard and needless work, only to wait till the next opportunity to run the logs.

Just then, Benning came down the hill, a lanky, knock-kneed figure in a floppy felt hat. He had light-gray eyes—so pale that they were nearly colorless—large reddish sideburns, and a devious face. Benning owned less woodland than Durlacher, but earned more from it. He had already been fined by the Landgericht in Schweinfurt for bribing a weirmaster to give his timber priority in being floated to the sawmills.

"Problem here?" he asked blithely. "Can I help?"

"Help?" Julius screamed. "This is all your doing. These trunks are more than seven meters long. Four meters eighty is the maximum, according to the rules."

"Aha, so Herr Gymnasiast has done his homework. Now, my boy, no Bavarian bureaucrat tells me what to do. Longer logs are more lucrative, plain and simple. And I thought: With a fellow like Konrad manning the gorge, everything'll be fine."

"So you think you can use men in my father's employ to drive your illegal timber?"

"Who says it's mine?"

Konrad and Julius turned their attention to a long pine that spun like a barrel without moving from its spot. There was no visible timber mark.

"In that case," Julius said, "they belong to no one. I'll just hammer in my father's mark." He took the stamping hammer from his belt and with a forceful blow, set Durlacher's mark, a *D* with antlers above it, into the log.

"Get your paws off my timber!" Benning bellowed.

But Julius ignored him and continued hammering.

Benning knocked his cap off.

Julius hammered his father's stamp into the next tree trunk.

Benning waded after him, grabbed him by the neck, and threw him into the water.

"Mr. Benning!" Konrad called.

"Stay out of it, boy," Benning replied without looking up. The tails of his long gray coat floated on the surface. "This is a matter between Durlacher and me."

Julius resurfaced, his blond hair stuck to his head. Benning took the hammer and threw it onto the bank.

"Had enough? Is it clear who's the boss around here?"

Julius was utterly shocked, nearer to tears than laughter, but he did not capitulate. Benning shoved his head underwater, as if drowning a cat.

Konrad picked up the hammer and said, "Let go."

Benning ignored him and maintained his grip.

Konrad swung with all his might, as though chopping down a tree, and struck Benning just above the knee.

On the sixteenth of May, all the men had assembled in the Wallreuth tavern following the annual procession in which the statue of Saint John of Nepomuk, the patron saint of skippers and rafters, was carried through the village. To be chosen to carry the statue was an honor and afforded the bearer a certain status. Nepomuk was made of sandstone and was hefty indeed. The bearers wore white shirts and wreaths of silvered oak leaves. Konrad wore that garland this year for the first time. Not so Julius.

Hinzpeter, who could not seem to get his beer stein replenished, despite him having laid it on its side in the customary manner, said, "If you lads order me a Weizen, then I'll tell you something most interesting. I heard it from the housemaid of the doctor who amputated Benning's leg. But I'm dying of thirst."

"I'll pay," Julius said, and gestured to the innkeeper.

Hinzpeter drank and took his time.

"Well, what did she say?" Julius asked impatiently.

"She said . . . that the doctor said . . . that on Benning's leg . . ."

"What?"

"That on Benning's broken leg, just above the knee, there was an enormous bruise. And that bruise had a very remarkable shape. It was a timber mark. The letter D with antlers above it."

The company fell silent. Hinzpeter lay his beer stein back on its side. All eyes were fixed deferentially on Julius.

Julius and Konrad glanced at one another.

Julius's eyes glided over Konrad's as lightly as water glides over stones, and he said to the others, "Yes. That's so. I had no choice. Anyone who tampers with our timber will have me to deal with. I felled him with my father's hammer."

It was March and the Wilde Rodach, running high from rainfall and thaw, did its name justice. Whereas for the rest of the year it was no more than a creek, and at times had so little water that the cattle had to go all the way down the banks to drink and a child could jump over it, it was now at its prime, a broad and mighty river. It stormed through the Franconian countryside like a regiment in gleaming armor, eager to be united with the larger division of the Rodach and then that of the Main; it picked up the hastening troops of the Thiemitz and the Lamitz, and carried them along in a triumphant march to the Rhine and, finally, the open sea.

As soon as the water began to rise, the number of women praying at the sandstone statue of Nepomuk increased. But having watched her eldest son drown on his very first turn as a raftsman, still in town, near the weir beyond the bridge, Konrad's old mother no longer prayed to Saint Nepomuk, but only to the Virgin Mary herself.

The water continued to rise. These were stormy spring days, and dark clouds followed the water's westward path. The largest trunks, intended for Würzburg, Frankfurt, Cologne, and Holland, began their journey.

Durlacher's logs waited three miles upstream, on the open spot on the bank where the horses had dragged them.

The men waded in the calm, ice-cold brown water in between the soggy grass and the rushing current, lashing the huge trunks together into rafts. These consisted of seven, nine, or eleven trunks—the longest, called "the king," in the middle, and the rest in descending lengths on either side. Even though he did not have hip boots, Konrad waded into the water to help.

By afternoon the rafts were assembled.

Durlacher climbed onto his horse, a dappled white mare that had been dozing in the bushes all morning. "Schramm, you'll go first. Then Hinzpeter. Then the Halders. We'll come back for the rest tomorrow."

"*Gotts Noma,*" said Schramm—this was Franconian for "in God's name"—as they pushed his raft into the current. The silver-crested stream pulled it along; old Schramm with his long peavey seemed hardly fit enough for the task, but he had done it for more than forty years without a single accident.

"Gotts Noma!" cried Hinzpeter and, as always, steered his raft downriver with nothing but his feet, like a circus acrobat on the back of a dark-colored horse, his pike nonchalantly in one hand, the other hand holding his cap high against his side, as he full-throatedly sang, *"Ich bin der Fürst der Wälder."*

"Go on, Georg and Michael. And mind, you're standing atop a fortune. Watch out for the rapids just beyond the ruins—it's a nasty spot and things have gone badly there before."

"Yes, sir," the brothers answered, as though from a single beard. "Gotts Noma."

"Konrad," said Durlacher, "you bring the equipment down. I don't trust Benning's men. I'll see you in the village."

"Yes, sir," Konrad said.

Durlacher's mare cautiously began the descent. Her rider attentively followed every swing of her bony haunches.

Konrad ran down the path to the ruins, at the most dangerous bend in the river. He threw down his bundle and pushed his way through the thicket. The water glinted through the dark pine branches. He was just in time to observe how Hinzpeter took the rapids: maneuvering almost nonchalantly, he stepped from one trunk to the other, steering with his weight. The raft shot into the mass of churning water, the back end fanned up out of the foam like the tailfin of a huge fish, and for a moment it appeared as though Hinzpeter, submerged up to his hips and his peavey raised level above his head, traveled upright through the water as if by magic. The raft resurfaced, water ran off the timbers as if from the flanks of the *Nautilus* that had braved the depths. Hinzpeter waved briefly with his cap, then put it back on, as though to acknowledge the applause of an unseen audience.

Konrad slung his gear over one shoulder and ran further down the path to follow Hinzpeter's journey. He panted and was dripping with sweat. In front of him, on the narrow wooded path, Durlacher descended slowly on his horse.

It wouldn't do to overtake his boss. He slowed his pace and followed the rider and horse. He noticed that the mare was missing a horseshoe. Her yellowish tail swept back and forth, right in front of his face. Durlacher had stuck his feet deep into the stirrups and was smoking a cigar. Their descent was torturously slow. Konrad adjusted his pack. Meanwhile, Schramm, Hinzpeter, and the Halder brothers sailed down the river, out of sight.

"You all right?" Durlacher asked, half turning back, a hand on the cantle. "Cora can carry some of it, if you need her to."

"No, thank you, sir," Konrad replied, "I'm fine."

As soon as the path widened, he asked, "Mr. Durlacher, may I pass? I'd like to watch them sail into town."

"Oh?" Durlacher said, kicking Cora's flank with his boot until she moved off to the right.

Konrad sidled past them.

"I've got a pair of hip boots for you," Durlacher said. "You can sail with Schramm until Hallstadt."

Konrad couldn't believe his ears.

"Actually, I've got enough rafters already," Durlacher added gruffly. "This is Julius's doing."

"Thank you, sir," Konrad said.

"Let's see if you're up to the job. Schramm will fill me in later. There's no room for you on the wagon, so you'll have to walk back."

"Yes, sir," Konrad said. No distance that he'd be allowed to raft was too great to walk home.

"I don't know if the boots will even fit you. Might be far too big."

"No problem, sir. I can pack them with wool. Thank you ever so much."

Konrad burst into a run, the hammers and axes dancing on his back and the saws swinging in his hands.

Just as he emerged from the woods, the Halder brothers were mooring their rafts.

Although Konrad was, according to his mother, the handsomest boy in all of Wallreuth, the girls would not give him the time of day.

Who would marry whom was a foregone conclusion. The May festival, where the village youth swung around the linden tree to the sound of the drum, violin, and bugle, was simply a public confirmation of what had already been settled upon. The prettiest girls married up, and the others had to settle for any man they could get. And Konrad was destined to be one of those men, even though he danced as well as Julius.

Julius was now enrolled at university, the first young man from Wallreuth to have made the grade. He wore an elegant gray suit with a white carnation in the buttonhole, and took turns dancing with all the girls in the village. He played the "man of the world" with consummate charm; the tittering girls swooned in his arms and allowed him to lead the dances, even though they knew full well that the Durlacher heir was destined for someone above their station.

There was even talk of an aristocratic fiancée, and someone said that they'd heard he was to go to America.

Konrad reckoned that, if nothing else, he would probably end up marrying Evchen. She was blind in one eye and tended the geese. He didn't even know if she could cook or was capable of carrying on a conversation.

They released Schramm's raft, which was still tethered to the shore, and it plunged sideways into the current, like a playing card being flicked into play.

"Only do anything if I tell you to, boy," old Schramm said over his shoulder. He undid the ropes and pushed off. "I'll be happy if you just don't fall overboard. Can you swim?"

"Never tried," Konrad replied.

He stood, legs apart, at the center of the raft. The pike he held flat in his hands was as wide as the river.

Schramm took his time lighting his pipe, the smoke wafting in Konrad's face. The raft glided down the middle of the river, as stable as a floating house. The girls on the shore waved to them. His mother had stayed home. They approached the bridge. The stone vault arched above them, dark and moss-covered; the sounds changed, the rush of the river was reduced to an echo, and Schramm used his pike for the first time, guiding the raft's tip away from the brickwork. The raft leaned forward, righted itself, and glided further. They were now past the spot where his brother had drowned. It had gone by so quickly that Konrad didn't even have time to check whether there were onlookers on the bridge.

Schramm glanced back and said, "You all right?"

Konrad stuck up his hand jovially, as if to say: "Of course I'm all right, what did you expect?"

They came to a spot where the river widened and flowed with apparent calm between high, wooded shores, like a frothy-mouthed horse champing at the bit but holding back for the time being. The horse's strides became longer as the valley opened up and the woods made way for meadowland. Far ahead of them, the Halder brothers sailed on an even larger raft, and, with no need to steer for the time being, they had sat down.

The clouds spread across the sky, as though they, too, wanted to make the most of the open space. On the horizon Konrad saw the steeple of a church he'd never seen before, and thought: I'm further from home than I've ever been. But it might just be the way the river meandered. They couldn't be that far from Wallreuth yet, because just then he spotted Evchen, the girl who tended the geese. She sat leaning against an alder, or rather, she lay there, probably asleep, her skirts hitched up to her waist and her legs spread. Her geese were more watchful than she—they scuttled about, necks extended, issuing cautionary honks. Evchen sat up, a twig in her hand. She looked their way but did not appear to see them. Maybe she was even blinder than he thought.

"Hardly sees a thing anymore," Schramm said, and whistled with his fingers.

Evchen walked to the shore and stood up to her bare ankles in the mud, surrounded by squawking and hissing geese, twisting their heads in unison to keep an eye on the raft. She, too, looked to one side, but with her blind eye toward them. She was distracted because Hinzpeter, who drifted about a hundred meters behind, had also whistled and made an obscene up-and-down gesture with his hand on his pike.

"Evchen! It's me, Konrad!" he called. "I'm sailing to Hallstadt!"

Now she looked in his direction and raised her hand in a curious gesture, as though blessing something without quite knowing what it was.

"She can talk, you know," Schramm said, "but she almost never does."

"I'm sailing to Hallstadt!" Konrad shouted again.

Evchen turned toward him, unresponsive and motionless in the mud. The raft moved swiftly onward, and her face became like an illegible sign in the distance.

They arrived in Kronach that same evening. There was a bridge with three arches, much bigger and higher than Wallreuth's, but the passersby did not lean over the parapet to watch the rafts pass.

Schramm said that this was an everyday sight for the townsfolk. The houses were like palaces, their endless rows of gray roofs obscuring the hills on which they were built. Konrad thought there couldn't possibly be another city in the world to equal this one.

"Is that the gymnasium?" he asked, pointing to a building far up on the highest hilltop.

"No, blockhead," Schramm laughed. "That's Rosenberg Fortress."

The rafts were moored in a long row along a towpath just outside town. They had brought blankets and provisions and would sleep on their rafts. Twilight fell, the first stars already visible. They were the same ones he had seen the night before, so they couldn't be all that far from home. The row of trees along the towpath blocked the view of the city. The other men headed into town and instructed Konrad to keep a close eye on things. Hinzpeter tied on a red kerchief, and the Halder brothers wore hats that looked ridiculously small on their large heads.

"And remember," old Schramm called out, "don't go dozing off. There are gypsies about!"

Konrad sat down on a crate, and to kill time he started whittling a figurine out of a piece of wood. First he thought it would be a Madonna, but the more he whittled, the more it began to resemble a goose. That would be tricky. The neck had to be long and slender, and the wood was not very strong.

He was alert, should gypsies turn up, even though he had no idea what they might look like. Sounds wafted over from the city, but they were too far away to distinguish, although he thought he heard music now and then. The gurgling of the water that flowed between the logs, the plash of a carp: this, for now, was all he heard of the wider world.

It took Konrad four days to hike the distance they had traveled by raft in as many days. If he lost sight of the river, he asked for directions to Wallenfels, because of course no one had ever heard of the hamlet of Wallreuth. He had slung the hip boots that Julius had arranged for him around his neck. It was the longest journey he had ever made on foot, but he wasn't proud. He was headed in the wrong direction. The Rodach flowed toward him on its way to the faraway lands on which he now unwillingly turned his back. More rafts sailed downriver; he watched them with regret, like a pilgrim who sees others on their way to the destination he failed to reach himself. Each step was a step toward the past. The river left the somber Franconian forests behind, but he would be heading back to them.

Konrad was a strapping young man, long-legged and broad-shouldered; he cut such a fine figure in the high hip boots and the dark vest with the double row of shining buttons—the typical dress of a rafter—that a painter from Bayreuth once asked him to sit as a model. Like Hinzpeter and Schramm, he wore an earring. Rafters believed that wearing it kept the eyes sharp—and, of course, it also distinguished them from the other Franconians. Once on the water, as soon as he'd left his birthplace behind him, he would tie a red kerchief around his neck.

He was often chided for remaining unmarried. The pastor had even spoken, through the latticework of the confessional, of a sacred duty. Mothers of eligible girls would broach the subject, and for a while the girls themselves did their very best, until they found a man elsewhere—then he could breathe easy, until new girls reached marrying age.

He had half a dozen books, all of them by Jules Verne. Twenty Thousand Leagues Under the Sea *had been the first. Julius had given it to him while he was still at the gymnasium. The title had confused him at first. No ocean, he thought, could possibly be twenty thousand leagues deep. He read it, year in, year out. Everything in it seemed of such inestimable value to him that it would suffice for an entire lifetime. The cover was blue and gold, in relief, like the pews in church. The illustrations were works of true wonder. One showed Captain Nemo, his arms folded, standing at a crystalline porthole and watching a gigantic octopus attack the* Nautilus. *On another, the caption (for there was always a sentence from the book underneath) read: "The Crew Attends an Underwater Funeral." The incredible precision of the engraving boggled his mind. Not only were all the characters represented in typical attitudes, so that one would readily recognize them—the dramatically protruding beard of the seaman, the bald head of the anxious scientist—but every illustration consisted, right to the very edge, of a dense network of meticulously drawn lines, executed with a perfection that Konrad, who whittled and carved his figurines with the tip of his pocketknife, would never achieve.*

He read and reread his six books at the kitchen table by candlelight, after having slid aside his plate of mashed potatoes and bacon.

Michael Strogoff: The Courier of the Czar *was the reason the little wooden goose he'd made during his first rafting journey in Kronach had no eyes. He was just about to burn tiny black eyes into the wood with a glowing ember when he recalled that the cruel Tartars had blinded Strogoff with white-hot steel, after which he could not bring himself to do it.*

By now the Main had become a familiar waterway. Konrad knew every mile and every vista. The hilltops and woods, here approaching and there receding from the riverbanks, the mouths of the tributaries, the bridges and the hillside vineyards, the grand plains, the fortresses, the wide bends, and the erratic way in which the stream meandered now northwest, now due south into the sun. The Main told a story he experienced time and again. Just like he read the Jules Verne books, he read and reread the Main.

He stood tall, his legs firmly planted, his peavey in both hands in case it was needed. Where the Main was calm, he walked back and forth along the lashed-together logs that drifted downstream under his feet, and enjoyed the breeze that made his shirt flap. Although with each new journey his raft was another raft, it always reminded him of the previous one, just as a dog reminds you of the dogs you'd had before it.

The Main was channeled now and flowed more slowly than it used to. It was a calm, dammed-up waterway that ran from east to west through the heart of Germany. It was no longer quite the same river he had dreamed of as a boy. But then again, when his old mother had started failing, he didn't love her any less either.

All that was left of those days was the brief spectacle when one passed the newly built dams and barrages, which invariably required a minute of steersmanship. But in between, nothing was the same anymore.

What also irked him were the steam trains and the automobiles in ever greater numbers, as though to drive home the fact that the days of rafting were over. And he was irritated by the heavy chain at the bottom of the Main, which pulled steamboats and other ships upstream and which Konrad thought unnatural. The chain ran from Bamberg to Kitzingen. The captains never yielded to the rafts, but rather seemed to intentionally ram into them, like the barbaric vanguard of a new age.

He found Evchen in a meadow not far from the village, and again she lay sleeping under a tree. He pitied her. She would never find a husband, now that she was getting older and was practically blind. She would spend her life tending geese in the fields around Wallreuth, and in the end she would have to rely on alms. The pastor preferred not to see her at Mass. Queer, racy stories about her made the rounds; they weren't even real stories, as though she wasn't worth them, but rather offhand insinuations from which Konrad concluded that she'd had just about all the men in the village.

He lingered in the bushes and looked at her, his hand clutching the wooden figurine in his coat pocket. His smooth, eyeless wooden goose suited no one better than her.

Morning mist still hung above the grass, lighter than the gray smoke that rose from Wallreuth's chimneys beyond the woods. A bend in the river glistened in the distance.

Her bare feet were drab from mud, and her legs were spread. Her skirt was an apron of clay. He did not look at her legs, for it gave him the same uneasy feeling he'd had at the sight of his mother, who, old and doddering and in her last months, indifferent to propriety, would sit, spread-legged, on the edge of her bed or squatted above the chamber pot with her nightgown hitched up.

Evchen's hands lay resigned and reflective in her lap. She wore a ragged and weedy straw hat; from under it came two thick, braided tresses, blonder than the hair of most of the local women, and he noticed that she had once—last year, perhaps—woven daisies into them, but now all that was left were dead, gray stems and desiccated buds.

He stepped out of the shrubs and carefully placed the little goose on her lap.

Before he could retreat, she opened her eyes, maybe because the guard goose had seen him and let out a warning honk; they were immense, blue-gray eyes that looked straight at him.

"Who's there?" she asked. "Heinrich, Georg, Hannla, Fritze?"

"It's me. Konrad. I've brought you something."

She felt the figurine with her fingertips, bowed her head slightly, and then said something most strange.

"Konradin," she whispered, "where our bed was, there you will find broken flowers and grass."

"What?" he asked.

She did not answer. The geese approached, hissing reproachfully.

"I wanted to give you this before I left. See you later this summer, Evchen."

"No one will know of us, except you and I. And a silent little bird."

"What a funny girl you are. Farewell."

Konrad had been working for Durlacher for seven years now, and the company had grown a great deal since Julius became junior partner. They had bought up all Benning's woodlands when he went bankrupt.

It was a fine, sunny day. Julius sat on the crates, smoking a cigarette and updating his ledger. This time the trunks were huge, more than twenty-four meters long. Stacks of sawn planks were tied to the rafts, as well as bundles of thinner trunks for the vineyards at Escherndorf and Sommerach. They also transported woven baskets and crates of eggs and vats of Franconian beer, which would be brought to market along the way.

It was Julius's idea to use the rafts to haul cargo, to make them cost-effective. His bicycle, an Excelsior Kavalier, went along as well: sometimes he would ride ahead to promote his wares here and there, and if Konrad saw him on the shore surrounded by buyers, he knew he had to moor.

A first lark hovered, unseen, high above the cornfields near Hetzfeld, singing joyously. The Excelsior Kavalier sparkled. Konrad imagined Julius as Columbus, and he himself at the helm of his flagship. Not that there was much left for him to discover on the Main: it eventually emptied into the Rhine, and the Rhine was the biggest, broadest river in the world; it flowed majestically past knightly fortresses and mighty mountains and was home, even to this day, to sirens whose enchanting song lured men like them to ruin. And then the Rhine left Germany, flowing to lands where they spoke another language; Schramm had told him that in the Low Countries, it branched into no fewer than eight rivers, each with its own name, on whose shores stood those fabulously wealthy Dutch cities, Haarlem, Herzogenbusch, Gouda, and Dort, all of their foundations built on Franconian tree trunks.

"Julius!" Konrad called.

Julius looked up.

"The Lohr weir."

Julius nodded, closed his book, and climbed atop the stack of crates. He wore mid-calf, lace-up shoes, sturdy enough to maneuver safely on the raft but not too heavy for pedaling on the bicycle, and proper enough to wear during business negotiations. Konrad was always amazed by the extent of Julius's wardrobe. He seemed to have a different outfit for every occasion, all of it as elegant as it was practical. A linen shirt with ironed pleats and a mole-fur vest for at the *Stammtisch*, the regulars' table, at the Krone. A vulcanized cape in case of rain. In the winter, a long overcoat with a herringbone motif and lambskin hat and gloves. In autumn, if the temperature dropped even a few degrees, Konrad saw him in a different suit and with a different overcoat than the day before; sometimes he even suspected that Julius chose his wardrobe to befit the colors of the season. He had money enough, of course. But there was something elusive and esoteric about Julius. That was perhaps what bound them: they each had something that distinguished them from the others in Wallreuth. But that something also kept them from knowing each other.

The raft pitched into the rapids, expertly steered by Konrad; a few passersby stopped on the bank, undoubtedly hoping for some mishap to gawk at. But with Konrad, nothing ever went wrong. The raft glided into the frothing depths and partially disappeared underwater. Julius ducked elegantly under the arch of the bridge, as self-assured as a preacher on his pulpit; then it was Konrad's turn to duck and then right himself to keep his raft on course for the remainder of the rapids, until a few seconds later all was calm again.

Julius stepped off the stack of crates, his feet still dry, and waved to him as he sat back down, opening the ledger to the spot he'd marked with his finger.

More passed between the two young men on this trip than Konrad had expected.

At Ludwigsbad, where he had cycled ahead, Julius awaited him not in the company of farmers or tradesmen purchasing planks or baskets, which they had in good supply, but of a young lady. Konrad did not think her particularly attractive or even hale, but she was undeniably elegantly dressed, and upon being introduced to her, it was clear that, for the first time in his life, he was in the company of nobility. Her name was Thekla von Wiedenhausen.

Julius informed him that she would join them on the raft for a short distance. In Volkach they would catch the steamboat back. He would leave his bicycle in Ludwigsbad so that the rafts could continue on their way without losing any time, and he would soon catch up with them.

This was a calm stretch of the Main, and the journey went without incident. Julius sat with his companion on the stack of crates at the front of the raft, and Konrad stayed at the back, so as not to overhear their conversation. Julius pointed out landmarks—the Klingenberg, the Vogelsberg—and she listened and occasionally held on to her hat when a breeze passed. The hat had a sky-blue ribbon that fluttered charmingly. She sat up very straight, and Konrad had plenty of time to take her in. From the back, his impression of her improved considerably. The summer outfit with its tailored jacket was very flattering indeed. The wide white skirts made it look like a swan had alighted on the crates to watch over the Wallreuth eggs.

Julius, too, sat upright in a somewhat studied attitude. Konrad imagined he was witnessing the first meeting between Julius Durlacher and his future bride. It was about time, for Julius was, like him, still a bachelor.

In Volkach, Julius announced he would take his lady friend for a walk up the hill to the famous pilgrimage church of Maria im Weingarten. He might therefore only join up with Konrad the following day, as Julius never slept on the raft but in the same set of inns his father had always frequented when traveling on business.

Konrad lay on his back and gazed up at the stars. The night sky was cloudless and nearly black. The stars were not his friends: for him, they had always symbolized changelessness, and what did not change was not good for him. As things stood, all that changed was himself, simply because he was getting older, which was no great achievement, it happened to everyone. Up until now, he felt, he hadn't accomplished much. He had been born, just like Napoleon, Beethoven, and Jules Verne, but that was where the similarities ended.

He slept fitfully, and awoke at every movement in the vicinity of the raft, no matter how small. If an owl flew over, he heard it. If the wind picked up or changed direction, he noticed it. If the monotone gurgle and slosh of the water underneath him was interrupted, even for a second, he would stay awake until he figured out what had caused it. Even a shooting star made him open his eyes, though it was usually gone by the time he looked.

And so he noticed a distant light that approached along the riverbank. It wobbled and weaved erratically. He knew right away that this will-o'-the-wisp was the carbide lamp of Julius's Excelsior.

Julius was drunk. He tossed his bicycle into the bushes and teetered onto the raft. I hope he doesn't break an ankle, Konrad thought.

"Your lamp," he said, because it was still burning, and needlessly lit up the shrubs.

"Forget it," Julius muttered, sitting down beside him.

Konrad pulled his blanket closer around him, so as not to catch a chill.

"What did you think of her?" Julius asked. "Thekla, I mean."

Konrad paused while considering his answer. He did not know what feelings Julius might have for her. He didn't find her pretty, but on the other hand, her manner when she'd been on the raft had made a good impression.

"I thought she was . . . elegant."

"She is. But that's not the point."

"What is the point, then?" Konrad asked.

Julius chuckled and stood up to go get the carbide lamp from his bicycle after all. He tripped and nearly fell between the raft and the bank. Something was going on with him, a conflict, but Konrad could not put his finger on it. He'd gone to fetch the lamp because it was senseless to let it burn, but something else was at play, something mercurial.

Another falling star—but he looked too late to make a wish.

Julius sat back down next to him and set the lamp aside.

There was something about Julius's face. It was regular and well formed, you might call it handsome, but it was nothing out of the ordinary. It was slightly round and diffuse. It was not the face of a man who knew where he belonged. It was half-peasant, half-gentleman. Maybe even half-man, half-woman.

"I took her up to the Maria im Weingarten," Julius said. "But that was just a ruse, and we both knew it."

Konrad said nothing. If Julius had something to tell, that was up to him, but it was not for Konrad to ask.

Julius was still for a while, as if waiting for a reaction.

"I had her," he said after some time. And when Konrad still did not respond, he offered details. "You know what, status and breeding don't mean a thing. A woman is a woman. The only difference is that with a 'lady,' there's a lot more underwear to sort out. D'you have any idea what all she had on under those skirts?"

Konrad did not know, and did not want to. What he did know, from the very start, was that Julius was lying.

He had not slept with Thekla von Wiedenhausen, and what he now told Konrad was perhaps his way of dealing with the disappointment. At the stammtisch in the tavern, Konrad had heard plenty of men boast of their conquests, and somehow he always knew whether it was the truth or just bravado. Green as he was, he never took part himself.

Julius laughed and laid a hand on Konrad's blanket. "Well, that's human nature for you . . . we are what we are. Doesn't it ever get to you? Unmarried and alone on the Main for months at a time?"

"No," Konrad answered.

Julius quickly withdrew his hand.

"Oh . . . Well, I'm bushed. Not much chance of me finding lodgings in Volkach at this time of night."

"Here, take my blanket," Konrad said, getting up. "It'll be getting light in an hour, and we have to push off on time."

Julius did not answer. He lay motionless on his back, half on Konrad's sack of straw and half in the gap between two trunks. His eyes were open, but he appeared not to see anything.

The next day, on the way to Würzburg, Julius was somber and moody. He drank too much last night, Konrad thought, and isn't used to sleeping in the open. Maybe that was it. Julius sat, sulking, hour after hour, on the stack of crates, facing backward.

"Don't stand up," Konrad warned. "Bridge."

"Don't tell me what to do, man," Julius said hoarsely, and added, once under the shadow of the stone arch, "I know better than you, you hick."

"Yes, Mr. Durlacher," Konrad replied, which was the most brazen thing he had ever said.

"You know, I've got a good mind to sack you," Julius said.

Just after the bridge came a narrow bend, one of the few moments the rafter had to take control of steering the craft. Konrad walked to the bow, toward Julius, his peavey raised.

"Don't you dare!" Julius shouted as he got up.

"What?" Konrad yelled back as he rammed the pike into the riverbed next to the outermost trunk, grasped it with both hands high above his head, and dangled from it. The water frothed in protest as the raft glided past the pike, which acted as a wedge, and swung sideways through the inside bend. As

Jules Verne's Robur the Conqueror said: "Give me a lever and I will move the world."

He became a hero on his twenty-third birthday.

The Great War was raging, and Julius fought as a reserve lieutenant in France.

Konrad had not volunteered, as fighting was not in his nature, and besides, men were needed to keep the logging business going in support of the war effort. Women could be put to work at the grenade and ball bearing factories in Schweinfurt, even half-blind ones like Evchen, who had been assigned there. But they couldn't chop down trees and drive timber.

The men in the Krone paid courteous attention to what little Julius had to say about his experiences at the front. He had become gaunt, and his eyes, once dullish, now glowed as if he had a fever. He was on leave and was due to return to his regiment, stationed on the Marne, in a few days. Hinzpeter was listed as missing; everyone assumed he was dead.

"The Marne?" old Schramm asked excitedly. "But isn't that where we made mincemeat of those Frogs? At Villiers?"

"That was the last war," Julius said, and mumbled something about reconnaissance balloons, reinforcements from the east, and an upcoming offensive, but it wasn't much more than they already knew from the *Bamberger Tageblatt*. Eventually he shrugged indifferently, as though there really wasn't that much to tell about the war, and then kept to himself.

"I'm proud of my son," Durlacher said, putting his arm over his shoulders, "and of his Iron Cross. Men, a toast to Julius!"

"To Julius!" they all said before drinking.

Ekkehart stood up and ticked a fork against his beer stein. With a tug he straightened his vest, with its eighteen gleaming buttons. The tabletop reached no further than halfway up his thighs.

"Gentlemen. Fellows. Mr. Durlacher," he began pompously.

"Come on, Ekkehart, out with it," Durlacher prodded. "What've you got to say?"

"What I have to say is a story. It is a tale of mettle and manliness. It's about the feat of a young rafter, far from the front."

"Mettle and manliness, that's what the fatherland needs, now more than ever," Durlacher said. "Do continue. Or should I say, begin."

Ekkehart placed his hands behind his back, as if there they might do the least harm, and frowned. Apparently he had learned the first sentences of his speech by heart: "Since time immemorial, the Main has been the domain of us rafters. Even in the days of the late, great Emperor Barbarossa, it was so. Our family tree is composed of trees."

"Bravo!" exclaimed Heinrich Halder.

"Everyone is familiar with the heroic deeds of our imperial army," Ekkehart continued, "but today I wish to commemorize a deed of heroism that took place far behind the front, but which likewise deserves a place in the annals . . . the annals . . ."

"Of Wallreuth?" Durlacher offered.

"Annals of Wallreuth, yes indeed, Mr. Durlacher, thank you kindly."

Just past Hallstadt they had encountered the inevitable steamboat, slogging its way upriver with five barges in tow. Due to the variable winds and the bends of the Main, the tow-boat blanketed the green hills on either side of the river with tufts of smoke, like a ruler of the underworld dragging his drab cloak over the faces of mortals he has subjugated.

In front of Durlacher's rafts was a small boat, rowed by a fourteen-year-old boy and flying a warning flag.

Red Peter, the captain of the steamboat, was thus warned and had time and space enough to move over, but he did not do so. He plowed with a derisive whistle signal straight up the middle of the river, although the rafts—a hectare of timber, stretched out over hundreds of meters—could not possibly yield. The little rowboat got caught up in the bow wave and capsized, flag and all. The steamboat rammed the first raft and rent it like a matchbook. Old Schramm fell overboard.

Konrad's raft was next in line.

Why is he telling them this? wondered Konrad. Everyone knows the story, except Julius. He did not feel like a hero. He had managed to steer his raft diagonally to the current just in time. He watched the bridge of the steam tug pass, a riveted bastion, and saw the jeering mugs of Red Peter and his crew. As the towboat passed, its bow wave pushing him further aside, he saw the cable that pulled the first barge dip underwater and then draw itself taut. Bischberg, on the far shore, was obscured by the gray clouds of smoke. He grasped his peavey in both hands, ran toward the passing steamboat, and jumped.

It's my birthday, he thought, high in the air, at the top end of his pike.

He landed squarely on the rear deck of the towboat, saw the tar in the crevices, and looked up at the astonished faces peering through the rear window of the riveted fort.

"And so, fellows, gentlemen, Mr. Durlacher, Lieutenant Durlacher—so did a man from Wallreuth single-handedly enter the enemy fleet."

Konrad stared into his beer stein. Why did he have to bring this up while Julius, who had gone through far more than anyone here, kept to himself? It was cheap, this kind of praise. He even recalled a certain disappointment at the moment he realized he was capable of the sort of heroism he had only known from the Jules Verne books. Being a hero wasn't anything special after all.

"He dragged Red Peter out of his wheelhouse and flung him over the railing. But also . . . what's more and additionally . . ."

"The towing lines," Heinrich Halder prompted.

"Right you are. With the audacity of a Von Spee or a Störtebeker, he brought the towboat to a halt and threw loose the towing lines!"

The men drummed on the table and cheered.

The next rafts passed to the side, and at the sight of the giants Halder and Ekkehart entering their vessel, the rest of the crew leapt overboard. The victory was complete. The rowboat with the signal flag was recovered, and Schramm and the shivering boy were scooped out of the water.

The fleet continued its journey under glorious summer clouds. They triumphantly passed the barges that Konrad had unleashed to the river.

"And where is the enemy's flag?" yelled old Schramm, who had already had too much to drink, and pulled a pennant of the Wulff Steamboat Company from his pocket. "Here is the enemy's flag!" he cried, and blew his nose in it.

Men got up to clap Ekkehart on the shoulders, and he sat back down, much satisfied, and emptied his beer stein in a single swig.

The whole table broke into song, the same one they had sung that day on their rafts so loudly that it echoed between the hills to their left and their right: *"Lieb Vaterland, magst ruhig sein! Fest steht die Wacht, die Wacht am Main!"*

Only Julius and Konrad did not join in.

Later, Konrad got up to look for Julius, who had been absent for some time. His uniform cap and Sam Browne belt were still hanging on the coatrack, so he couldn't have gone home. He first checked the latrine in the dark courtyard behind the Krone, but it was empty. The inn's shutters were closed, but the laughter of the men at the stammtisch still echoed its way outside. It was a hazy night, so not many stars were out. He thought for a minute, then walked for about fifty meters down the narrow path that ran between the beanstalks and cornstalks on its way to the riverbank. He saw the red glow of a cigarette. Konrad had noticed earlier that Julius, who never smoked before, now lit up one after the other.

"Konrad," Julius said flatly, as if to simply state a fact.

"Yes."

"Cigarette?"

They smoked in silence.

"That was uncalled for," Konrad said. "Ekkehart's story about my so-called heroism."

"Never mind," Julius said apathetically.

The bitter cigarette was not round but flat. "Turkish?"

Julius nodded. A few minutes later he said, "The world will never be the same, you know, after this war."

"You mean the steam towboats?" Konrad asked after some reflection.

"Those too," Julius replied, and flicked his cigarette butt into the darkness. "I'm heading home. I have to leave tomorrow morning at five, to be at the station on time."

"Good night. Look after yourself."

"Sure thing," Julius said, and vanished into the darkness.

Konrad stayed there for a long time, as if waiting for the void Julius left behind to fill up on its own, like the murmur of the Rodach returned after the fickle wind had temporarily stolen it, like the stars overhead revealed themselves after a cloud had passed. But this did not happen. It felt as if he'd lost a friend, even though he and Julius had never been close in the first place.

Konrad stared at the river. Something moved near the reeds, an eel perhaps. The wind had died down completely. A few stars were reflected in the water, which was as dark as black glass.

The Rodach, the Main, and the Rhine: the one flowed into the other and ended in the same sea. But other streams that never met also emptied into the same sea.

The raft was enormous. They had spent days assembling it, and with the foremen's instructions, it continued to grow as more and more segments were added, until the Höchst harbor basin was one huge expanse of timber, and the foremost tip already jutted into the river, like a gigantic birthling struggling out of its mother's womb. Straightening his back to wipe the sweat from his forehead, Konrad saw a forest of chimneys and cranes. Hour after hour, day after day, he did as instructed, and what he had done his entire life: lash tree trunks into a raft. But this time he had lost sight of his part in all this because whatever he did was at once conglomerated into a far larger whole, a monstrous wooden snake that gradually squeezed between the jetties and out into the river.

They would need dozens, if not hundreds, of men to steer this huge raft. Its destination was Holland, that much was clear, and all the trunks bore the Durlacher timber mark.

Provisions were brought on board: beer, cured meat, beans, fruit, potatoes, and preserves, as though they were headed, rather than for Rotterdam, for some faraway continent. There was even an oven so they could bake fresh bread underway. And on the morning of their departure, a train arrived with a shipment of wood panels, some already fitted with windows and doors, so a cabin could be constructed in the middle of the raft.

Julius arrived in his father's grand, gleaming Horch.

He got out and marched briskly to the quay to inspect the work being carried out under his authority. He wore a sporty brown-gray blended suit with plus fours and a flat English cap.

Konrad stood up straight, a hand on his back. To his surprise, Julius caught sight of him immediately among the dozens of men at work on the docks, raising an arm to wave at him.

"Konrad!" His voice had never been very powerful, so Konrad did not catch what was said, but Julius's gestures made it clear that he wished to speak to him. He excused himself from the others and crossed the expanse of wood. Julius had already extended his hand while Konrad's foot was still on the top iron rung.

"Hello there!" he exclaimed. "The time's come! Life can finally begin!"

Konrad was caught off guard and was somewhat wary. He hadn't seen or spoken to Julius in two full years.

"My father has made me his proxy, so I'm free to do business as I see fit. And as you can see, I don't go in for half measures. This is the first Durlacher raft to sail all the way to Holland. I've a deal with a harbor baron in Rotterdam."

"Good to see you again," Konrad answered.

"And surely you've heard that I'm to marry?"

"No," Konrad said. "Congratulations."

"The daughter of Melzer, of Melzer & Unruh from Schweinfurt. Ball bearings. A good match."

"What's her name?"

"Well, her sister's called Gloria, now that's a pretty name . . . her name is Hermine."

"Congratulations," Konrad said again.

Julius's eyes darted back and forth between the spar rafts in the harbor, Konrad's face, and the Horch. He couldn't stand still or keep quiet for even a moment. He talked nonstop, about the future of logging and international treaties; about his wedding, which would be consecrated by the archbishop of Bamberg; about the journey by car along the Main. Konrad stood there awkwardly, cap in hand. He wondered what he had done to deserve all this chumminess. Julius was still his old, unfathomable self.

"You're coming too, of course, Konrad . . . we're going to sail down the Rhine together! Damn them, they'll bang their barrow into my Horch yet . . . Hey, you there! Idiots!" And with that, he hurried off, leaving Konrad standing alone.

The Rhine. Konrad's head spun as he descended the steep iron ladder, only letting go of the rungs with one hand or foot at a time, and still holding on awkwardly to his cap, which he only realized when he'd reached the bottom. The Rhine. At last. It was going to happen.

He put on his cap, wiped the rust from his palms, and stepped onto the endless expanse of timber. Even in the brief time he'd been speaking to Julius, the raft had grown even larger. Incredible, that this wooden peninsula could go on a journey. By evening it was finished. It lay ready on the bank of the Main, four hundred meters long and more than forty meters wide.

The front end of the raft disappeared from view as the Main curved off to the north. Konrad saw the towers of the Mainz Cathedral and knew thcy had now reached the Rhine.

Despite the fine summer weather, Julius had retired to his private cabin to catch a few hours of sleep.

The Rhine was immensely wide; a gray-green expanse of water stretched out before him, and a long series of buoys marked off the sailing channel. Far to the west he could see blue hilltops, perhaps that was France. And there was ship traffic like he'd never seen before, going both up- and downstream. This really was the wide world. He saw steam towboats pulling barges loaded with ore, a snow-white passenger ship, two identical ferries that passed each other midstream. Down close to the shore was a bulky dredging operation. The hillsides were blanketed with vineyards from which ribbons of smoke rose and where all manner of machinery glistened in the sunlight. On the far side, a railway ran parallel to the river, and slightly below it, a highway followed the bank; a locomotive pulled a well-nigh endless string of freight cars behind it, and on the road, automobiles from opposing directions passed one another effortlessly. And he noticed a sound he had never heard before: the Rhine valley buzzed with the drone of nonstop activity. A life he never even knew existed seemed to be playing out here. While the sky was no different than above the Main, here, it mattered less—the white summer clouds were at most on a state visit; they did not dominate the landscape.

The Rhine was majestic, and Konrad noted with satisfaction that the others heeded their raft. The colossus that now nosed its way onto the Rhine forced the rest of the water traffic to yield to it.

"Something else, isn't it," Julius said, and laid a hand on Konrad's shoulder. "Unremarkable, mind you—but hardly an everyday sight for me either."

"This is it, Julius," Konrad said, his voice muted. "The Rhine."

"Yes, of course," Julius laughed. "The Rhine."

That evening they moored at Ingelheim. Braziers had been placed at intervals so that the men could find their sleeping posts. The raft was like a town with its own streetlights. It was so large that the glint of the river seemed like a distant sea.

Konrad went off on his own, his duffel bag slung over his shoulder, and walked to the foremost edge of the raft, so as to sleep as close as possible to the Rhine.

He sat down and put his hand into the cool current. He was a rafter who did the same work as thousands before him. It was nothing special, but still he knew he would never be happier than at this moment.

The lights of Ingelheim and those on the hillsides reflected in the dark water. The trunks under him were lined up smartly, like soldiers in formation recruited into foreign duty.

As a child he believed that Holland was actually built atop an underground Franconian forest. He imagined it grew upside down, like the trees reflected in the Wallreuth village pond, and supported the Dutch houses on its roots.

He felt in his jacket pocket for his tobacco pouch and matches. Whether and how much he slept was his own business. He was on the Rhine, and he was free. He didn't need a Russian revolution or a world war for that.

"Konrad?"

Julius bent over him. "You asleep already? Come to my cabin, I've got something to show you."

What was that all about? thought Konrad as he made his way back to his bunk in the middle of the night. All Julius did was talk and uncork one bottle after the other, pouring wine in a cut-crystal glass. Konrad was just glad he hadn't toppled or dropped it. Of course, Julius had showed off the electric lamp that ran on batteries, and his camp bed was covered with the pelt of a bear that he claimed to have shot while hunting with his father-in-law. But what did Julius want from him? Now that they were adults, they had nothing in common anymore. Julius was the boss and he was an employee, that was all. And besides, Konrad preferred beer to wine. In the course of the evening, he even felt put out, stuck there against his will; he had wanted to spend his first night on the Rhine on the edge of the raft, next to the river, not in those comfy quarters that had been built for Julius.

Julius had switched off the electric lamp as soon as Konrad left. He stepped cautiously over the sleeping figures wrapped up in their blankets. In the east, the first outline of clouds was beginning to show, a lone star still shone, like the head of a nail hammered shiny.

Suddenly someone grabbed his ankle.

"Did ya make him happy?" said an unctuous voice. "If you're in the mood for more . . . come and lie down."

Konrad did not know this man. He wasn't a rafter; he must've been one of the day laborers they'd hired back at Höchst.

But Konrad did not know himself either, for he did something he never thought he'd be capable of. He planted his hobnailed shoe on the man's face.

"Let go," Konrad hissed.

"Oh, like it rough, do you?" he heard from under his shoe. "So do I."

Konrad pressed his shoe even harder onto the face. The man released him, rolled onto his side, and grabbed his head in pain. Konrad wound up to give him a kick.

Here and there, men sat up in their bedrolls; in the dim light of the brazier, he saw on them the same kind of mug as on those Bolshevik ruffians who had stirred up trouble in Wallreuth after the war. Pleb faces, marked by hard labor and alcohol. They looked at him with a kind of drowsy disdain. There was something about him that aroused antagonism in this sort. Maybe that's what old Durlacher meant when he once told Konrad he had manners above his station. Right now he felt, in spite of everything, far more kinship with Julius than with these thugs.

He found his own bedroll, wrapped himself up, and fell asleep at once.

When he awoke to the sound of the Ingelheim church bells, he saw the unimaginably wide Rhine stream noiselessly past him under the lacy morning mist.

The first castles, high on the far-off hilltops, were not as impressive as he had expected, but his attention was focused on maneuvering his sweep, the steering oar that could be positioned at right angles to the current to control the direction of the raft. By now he knew that "Hessenland!" meant starboard and "France!" meant larboard. The pilot, standing on a wooden tower at the back of the raft, called out orders through a megaphone.

That he hardly noticed the knightly fortresses of his childhood dreams, and that most of them were no more than stumpy ruins, did not bother him. He was like a bridegroom who took his wedding night as it came, even if the bride did not live up to his expectations. This was the Rhine.

Julius walked back and forth in his white linen suit, a cigarillo clamped between his lips.

"How many men on board, Julius?" Konrad called out.

"A hundred ninety-eight, according to my register!" Julius replied, contented.

It was a nearly windless autumn day, and the huge raft passed the notorious Binger Loch with ease.

The rafters familiar with the river let out the occasional yell at places where they knew the hillsides would throw back an echo. A raft like this, which dominated the Rhine as far as the eye could see, and for which all other vessels yielded as it crept through the bends of the river, was one of the largest manmade movable objects on earth. No ocean liner could match it. They were one country en route to another.

The men howled and screamed loudest when they passed the Lorelei. This was an age-old custom in which they all participated. The aim was to rouse the comely nymph from her thousand-year slumber. It was more like a taunt: What threat could she possibly pose to a raft as powerful as theirs?

It must have been a combination of the amount of beer the men had drunk at midday and an error on the part of the pilot, for all the underwater rocks in this section of the Rhine had been charted centuries ago. Or maybe the obstacle was a recently-sunk barge.

The rear section of the raft took a curve too wide, swerved close to shore, and heaved upward as though lifted by a whale; the cords and yokes holding it together snapped, and the logs began to separate. Men fell into the gap; some managed to grab hold, like finches on a branch, and climb back onto the raft. The men in the middle section ran toward the rear, despite the shouts of the pilot for everyone to remain at his post in order to stay the course. The Lorelei was a gray, indifferent rockface. In their confusion they rescued those who did not need their help, while one man who had become wedged between the rolling logs, and had let go, was swept behind.

Julius darted across the raft like an athlete on his way to the Amsterdam Summer Olympics. To Konrad's amazement, he dove into the water with elegant form, hands in front and white shoes pressed together. For a moment he was visible under the surface—a fish swooshing away from the forward-charging raft—until the glare blocked their view.

Just as Konrad went to remove his shoes, Julius resurfaced with the half-drowned man in his arms. He grabbed one of the ropes dragging behind the loosened logs and was pulled in, hand over hand, with his catch.

It was the fellow who had harassed Konrad the previous night.

His face was still swollen and scratched, although this was the least of his problems: he was unconscious, and his legs, in his wide, drenched trousers, were bent at an unnatural angle. Konrad pumped the man's chest in an attempt to restore his breathing, but to no avail.

"Let me," said Julius, who had meanwhile retrieved his Panama hat. He knelt beside the victim and pressed his lips to the man's mouth, supporting himself on his elbow while also holding his hat up in the air, as though determined to keep it dry. It looked like a Charlie Chaplin film, Konrad thought: Charlie alternating between kissing his bride and gasping for air. None of the other men had ever seen mouth-to-mouth resuscitation before, and they watched skeptically, until the man took a first sputtering breath, and then resumed breathing entirely on his own.

Julius stood up and looked around haughtily. It was as though he'd been awarded the Nobel Prize, but turned it down. He put on his hat and jerked the brim straight. He glanced at Konrad with an expression that said, "You're not the only hero around here." And then off he walked, his hands on his drenched back. The men made way for him. The Lorelei had vanished from sight.

At Koblenz they were made to moor. Military men in blue uniforms, the French occupation forces, climbed on board to inspect the raft.

Julius had to present all the papers; freight and personal belongings were searched. That nearly all of the soldiers were Africans who did not speak a word of German evoked some resentment. Most of the rafters had never seen a black man before, and it irked them that these men were grabbling through their chests and duffel bags.

An enormous Senegalese held up the book Konrad had with him.

"Ah, Jules Verne," he said, smiling. *"Bon!"*

"Bon!" Konrad replied.

Now he had not only seen his first black man, but had spoken a foreign language for the first time besides.

Julius was impeccably polite and even drank a glass of schnapps with the officers. Konrad heard him converse with them in fluent French. For Konrad, it was like hearing a rooster suddenly coo like a dove. Some of the rafters were standoffish or hostile, while others attempted to fraternize with the exotic intruders fanning out over their raft. These were mostly the hirelings from Frankfurt and Höchst, not the Franconian rafters. But the Tirailleurs sénégalais would have none of it: they came as occupiers and would have no truck with the enemy they had defeated at the front.

Konrad put away *The Danube Pilot*, and, to distract himself, began carving a wooden figurine.

He heard Julius ask: "Douaumont? Reims?"

To which the other replied: "*Non*—Chemin des Dames . . ."

"Chemin des Dames, *mon capitaine*?" Julius exclaimed. "*Moi aussi*. I was with the Bavarian Division under General Boehn, at Hurtebise."

"Hurtebise? But . . . I say—Senghor, over here!"

The sergeant who had searched Konrad's gear went over and saluted. He was a sturdy giant, the blue tunic taut around his belly and broad, hollow back.

Konrad needed no knowledge of French to understand the exchange that followed.

"See here: my Croix de Guerre, monsieur."

"See here: my Croix de Fer."

That evening, Julius came to get him.

"Come with me, Konrad. I've a surprise for you. It's really special. Today's my birthday."

"How old are you?" Konrad asked.

"Forty—the same as you."

They walked the entire length of the raft, which was fixed to the quay only at its rearmost section, the rest stretched out downstream like a pier. It resembled a deserted nomad camp, now that most of the men were in Koblenz in search of diversion. The statue of Kaiser Wilhelm on horseback darkly guarded the confluence of the Moselle and the Rhine from its pedestal, but Konrad soon lost sight of it as he followed Julius up the steep alleyways leading to the nightlife district.

Julius had been drinking, this much was obvious, but he was not drunk. He was apparently eager to share something with Konrad and hurried as though whatever it was would not last for long. Konrad picked up his pace to keep up. The alleys became smaller and stank of piss and peril.

"Julius! How much further?" Konrad asked, out of breath. "What're we doing here?"

"Just a bit more," Julius replied. "We're almost there."

He stopped and pulled on a bell.

It was a nondescript house, but inside was another matter entirely.

A rotund woman received them in a small salon whose walls were decorated with deer antlers. She wore a low-cut satin-and-taffeta evening dress, and alongside her on the sofa, a young redheaded girl in her underwear sat, peeling an orange.

"Ah, you're back," the woman said. "They're still upstairs."

Julius beckoned him, and they climbed the stairs, as steep as the stairs in Holland were said to be, although this was only Koblenz. It smelled musty. Piano music wafted past.

Konrad hesitated. Stopped. "Julius."

"What?" Julius asked over his shoulder.

"I'm not sure I want to be here."

Julius laughed. "Come on, it's a friendly place. Didn't I say I had a surprise for you?"

"What kind of surprise?" Konrad asked, still stopped on the landing.

"Ach, buddy!" Julius stood there quite convincingly, a foot already on the topmost tread, and pointed his thumb upstairs. "Come along and I'll show you something of Wallreuth you've never seen before."

"Wallreuth's got no secrets from me," Konrad replied. "What could you have in there that I haven't seen?"

"Come with me, and you'll find out."

Konrad followed him upstairs. Maybe he shouldn't have, but he did. There were four or five doors in a row, shabbily painted, and while there wasn't much to see in the passageway, which was lit by just a small gas lamp, there was all the more to hear: the hiss of the lamp, groaning, stumbling, the creak of a bed.

"I don't want this," he said.

"Oh yes, you do," Julius whispered. "You will. Just you wait."

He opened one of the doors and pulled Konrad in behind him.

The first thing Konrad saw was the enormous Senegalese officer, his sky-blue uniform trousers dropped around his boots. And next he saw a naked woman perched on the edge of a rumpled bed.

"Here you are," Julius said in a coarse whisper as he shoved Konrad forward. "A souvenir of Wallreuth."

The woman, very pale and blond, had the black man's member in her mouth.

The man swayed rhythmically with his bottom half; he held his cap, his hand resting on his hip, as though this was no more than a brief interruption in his daily routine.

The woman, too, did what she did with a certain indifference, every so often brushing back her flaxen blond hair and gagging, as though executing an unsavory but familiar task.

"So what do you say now?" Julius gloated. "If you want a turn . . . I've paid for the whole evening!" He took off his coat and snapped the suspenders off his shoulders. "She's totally blind now, d'you see? Doesn't have a clue anymore what's getting put in her gob."

"*Merci*, Germans," said the Senegalese, grinning, as he pulled up his trousers.

"Come on, man, it's paid for," Julius said as the officer shut the door behind him. "Me first, then you . . ." He took her by her braid and pulled her head into position. "So did I promise you a good time, or didn't I?"

On the nightstand was the little wooden goose Konrad had given her.

"Konradin," Evchen whispered as she took Julius's member in her hand.

From downstairs he heard a chanson, accompanied by a piano—a gramophone, he guessed.

Without looking back, Konrad slammed the door behind him.

So it passed that Konrad walked along the bank of the Rhine, from Koblenz to Bonn and from Bonn to Cologne, in search of work, while the economic crisis spread across Germany and followed him wherever he went, like a stigma. The money he earned in one town was worthless by the time he reached the next one. A thousand-Reichsmark note barely bought him a loaf of bread. Fewer and fewer rafts were floated down the Rhine, so when he looked for work on the quays, he was rejected as soon as he showed his papers. Only the livestock was oblivious to the Depression. People, on the other hand, were distrustful and hostile and treated him as a vagrant. He carried his tall hip boots with him from village to village and from city to city; his pike was long gone, but the wrought-iron hook was still in his knapsack.

He stayed close to the Rhine, even though the river no longer supplied him with work. He sold his earring, and now he only took the red kerchief out of his pocket to blow his nose.

Konrad had to face the fact that he was no longer a young man. The truth hit him at the market in Dusseldorf. He was loading turnips onto a cart when a stunning young woman walked past with a bread basket on her arm.

"Whaddya gawkin' at, man!" the farmer he worked for yelled. "We gonna work today or not? Get a move on!"

"Do you know what's so bad about getting old?" Konrad asked.

"Yeah," said the farmer, "that I have to hire you to carry crates for me."

"It's not so much having to give up the things you used to have. It's the realization that there are things you'll never get."

"And so you're just going to sit there? You got back problems or something? When I hired you, you said you was fit."

"I just saw a pretty woman."

"These things happen," said the farmer.

"And I didn't think to myself: I'd like to have her. I thought, Wouldn't it be fine to have a daughter like that."

In the summer of 1931 he arrived in Duisburg, where there was a large timber entrepôt. If he didn't find work here, then he would have to resort to the Salvation Army soup kitchen.

Konrad worked alternately at the circular saw, the bark stripper, and the rail-mounted crane. In all those years, though, he'd hardly touched a tree trunk with his hands, and it seemed increasingly unlikely that he'd ever sail on a raft again. In the summer of 1933, his hand got caught in the circular saw, and he lost three fingers.

"You're no good with machines," his boss said. "From now on, you'll scrub logs. You can still hold a scrub brush, can't you?"

He earned less than ever, standing in a cement basin in his hip boots, scrubbing tree trunks by holding the brush between his thumb and index finger.

For a while he chastised himself for not being able to come up with an alternative to rafting. He recalled his mother once saying: "If you can do one thing, you can do another." Wise words indeed, but he had no other ideas and couldn't do anything else. It was as if long ago, perhaps that day when, as a boy, he was allowed to go to the woods to help drive timber, he made a lifelong decision. Neither he nor the Reichsmark could do anything about having become worthless.

One day a raft moored on their quay. It was pulled by a black towboat with an enormous swastika flag on the stern, and it was en route to Nijmegen with a cargo of German lumber.

The raft carried passengers too. Konrad had seen this before: emigrants for whom traveling by raft was the only affordable way to leave the new Germany. They paid the captain or ship owner under the table. After the lumber had been loaded, Konrad went onto the raft to feel the floating timbers under his feet once again. It was not a raft as he knew them. The logs were held together by iron crossbars, and the towboat pulled them on chains. It was a rigid contraption that couldn't move with the water, but this was probably a moot point as the raft was not at all large, six by sixty meters at most. It couldn't compare to the majestic one on which he and Julius had once sailed the Rhine.

He inspected the crossbars and the heavy metal rods that had been hammered through them. He stood with his back to the towboat, because the wind blew a heavy, stinking cloud of smoke over the raft.

The emigrants had brought suitcases, bags, and bundles. They sat, their eyes downcast, hunched over on their luggage. Their postures exuded resignation; if they harbored any hope of a better life, then they hid it well. None of them looked at the river that would transport them to a new fatherland. None showed any interest in the cranes and chimneys of Duisburg—like mourners ignorant of the gravestones surrounding them.

He recognized Julius at once. It wasn't someone who looked like him, it *was* Julius. He was bent over the waterlogged cardboard suitcase of a fellow passenger, trying to fasten it with his belt.

Julius suddenly looked up, as though he felt Konrad's presence behind him. He was nearly bald and wore gold-rimmed glasses. They greeted each other guardedly but soon realized the aloofness was only the fear that the other, after all these years, might still bear a grudge. They were glad to see each other.

The ropes were already being let loose as the towboat prepared to continue its journey. Konrad's boss appeared at the quay in his brown Sturmabteilung uniform and called out to him to return to shore. Despite the tall boots and the Sam Browne belt, he looked anything but formidable, with his bowlegs and paunch. There wasn't much time; they had to fill each other in on their fortunes in a few short sentences. Julius, being half-Jewish, had no place in the Third Reich and was planning to go to Holland. Konrad told of his life since Koblenz.

The last rope was untied.

Without looking up, Julius put a hand on his arm.

"Come with me to Holland," he said. "I've got some money. Enough to pay your passage, at least. You've got papers?"

Konrad placed his mutilated hand on his breast pocket and nodded.

"You remember that line from the Grimm fairy tale? 'Something better than death, we can find anywhere . . .' Come with me, Konrad."

Konrad turned and called to his boss, "I'm not coming ashore! I'm sailing down the Rhine!"

"You're penniless, you fool!" the boss yelled back. "Come back and get to work!"

"No!" Konrad shouted.

"Nobody else'll hire you!" The boss hobbled along the quay after the towboat. "You're uneducated and half-crippled, man! And you don't have a party membership book!"

Konrad did not answer. The man stood there at the end of the quay, and the chimneys, cranes, and silos of Duisburg soon disappeared behind the smoke of the towboat.

"I always knew we'd sail all the way down the Rhine together one day," Julius said when Konrad sat down beside him.

In Ewijk, just past Nijmegen, they moored the raft in a small inlet on the south side of the river, which was now called the Waal; there wasn't much more than a few sheds and woodpiles. This was Konrad's first time outside of Germany. Everything looked different here, even the poplars along the dike. The tow-boat turned, as though spurning Holland, and headed back. The west wind pushed the black exhaust fumes and the large swastika flag in its direction of travel.

They watched as the emigrants walked along the dike back to Nijmegen, where there was a train station.

"What now?" he asked.

"Now I'll make a phone call to my old associate in Rotterdam," Julius replied.

The nearest telephone was in a café in the village. When he returned, he shook his head. "New owner," he said, "who says he can't do anything for us."

They spent the night in one of the sheds. There was little activity in the port. The next day a two-horse cart came to fetch the lumber. No one seemed to know who the raft belonged to, and a week later it was still moored there. Julius eventually found out it was owned by a building contractor in Dordrecht.

He wrote to him in German and English, offering their services, but got no answer.

For the time being, they slept in the shed, counted the guilders Julius still had, and looked out over the broad and glistening river that flowed past them. They frequently inspected the raft, which they now considered theirs, until they had identified every last timber mark on the logs.

The contractor finally got in touch and offered them fifteen guilders to bring the raft to Dordrecht, which would save him the extra cost of a towboat.

That evening they stood together on their raft and made plans.

"The crossing to America costs more than I've got, even for second class," Julius said, "but maybe we can work our way across—washing dishes, for instance. That's how nearly all the millionaires in America started."

"America?" Konrad said. "I don't want to go to America."

"Where to, then?"

"Only to the end of the river."

"Suit yourself. Once we get to Dordrecht, you'll almost be there."

It had started snowing; a translucent whirlwind of snowflakes descended on the dark river.

"We'll be needing peaveys," Julius said. "And about three days' worth of provisions."

They walked back and forth over the logs.

"What happened?" Konrad asked out of the blue. "Why did you and your wife divorce?"

"Because she was better off without me. She had an *Ariernachweis*."

"I thought the Melzers were Jews too."

"They were. But her grandparents converted."

"And yours didn't?"

"Only my father. But that wasn't enough. I'm grateful he doesn't have to endure all this."

"Couldn't she help you after the divorce?"

"She could have. But it wasn't a good marriage," Julius said. "Let's leave in the morning."

That same evening, in the shed, Konrad took out the wrought-iron hook he had been carrying with him all these years and attached it to the tip of a long willow branch. Then he brought out his hip boots.

"I wouldn't bother with them," Julius said. "The Waal's a calm river, but if you fall in with those things on, you'll drown all the same."

But when we sail into Dordrecht, Konrad thought to himself, I'm putting them on.

Neither man slept much that night, and they heard every hourly chime of the Ewijk church bell.

At daybreak they undid the chains and pushed the raft out of the inlet and onto the river.

Konrad was vigilant, like a man who, after many years, meets up with a woman he once loved. After all, she went by another name and this was her country, not his; who knew what had become of her? She might be rancorous, unpitying, hurtful. But the river, broad and unambiguous, flowed smoothly between the flooded washlands and the snow-covered breakwaters. It wasn't cold, a few degrees above freezing, and there was hardly any wind. They could make out the blades of the windmills through the light snowfall. The cattle had already been brought inside; only a few sheep grazed along the dike.

"Keep to the edge of the channel," Julius had warned. "I'm not sure if the cargo ships'll give us right of way. They used to, but we're not on the big raft now."

Indeed, the first barge that overtook them did not yield, and Konrad steered outside the buoys. First the tar-black bow appeared, showing the name *Spes Bona*. The shipmate on the roof of the deckhouse signaled to the pilot, but even if he had wanted to steer clear, it was too late. Many meters of riveted steel glided past them; the tautness of their lashed logs made the raft bob dangerously. A decidedly ill-humored spitz trotted along the ship's gangway, keeping even with them for as long as the passage lasted. When the pilothouse passed, the captain opened the door and cried out, in Dutch: "Well, I'll be damned! A raft? I thought we were rid of those wretched things."

"Dankeschön," Konrad called back, ignorant of what the man had said.

The dog glowered at them from the poop deck, snowflakes sticking to its furry head. Like his master, he was not keen on a raft on their river, let alone a raft manned only by a fellow wearing a long black coat and a hat and another armed with a metal-tipped pike.

They read, under a faded Dutch tricolor on the stern, the unpronounceable place name *Gorinchem*.

"Maybe we should hoist a flag too," Konrad suggested. "If only to be a bit more visible."

"I wouldn't know which one," Julius replied.

"We'll stay outside the buoys," Konrad said. "The river's wide enough."

"Just tell me what to do. You're in charge."

"Go stand at the back and warn me if something comes along."

"Aye-aye, Captain," Julius said, and walked to the rear of the raft.

Every so often Konrad glanced over his shoulder. Julius stood stock-still, his hands on his back, as if he were not only surveying the river, but his entire past.

"By the way," Julius said that night, "I picked up Evchen in Koblenz, on the way back from delivering the big raft to Holland."

Konrad said nothing, and stoked the fire. It was too cold to sleep outside, and they hadn't found any shelter for the night. They had knocked at the door of a large farmhouse, but were not welcome. They would stay up and push off again at first light. From here, they could reach Dordrecht in one day.

"I wanted to take her back to Wallreuth. I offered her a job at my parents'. Housekeeping, or in the yard. I had to pay off the madam. Evchen still owed her rent."

Konrad tossed willow twigs onto the fire. They might be the property of the farmer who had turned them away, but he didn't care.

"We had to change trains at Frankfurt. I left her on a bench in the waiting room, and when I got back she was gone."

"Where'd you go?"

"To buy cigars."

"And you never saw her again?"

"No. And I don't think we ever will."

Daybreak. A skein of geese passed above the Waal.

Maybe she eventually found a man after all, Konrad thought, who would look after her.

Loevestein Castle loomed ahead.

"Just another hour or so until Dordrecht," Julius said. "Any idea how we'll get this thing into port?"

"You've done it once already."

"Come now. All I did was sashay around in my white suit."

Julius walked to the edge of the raft to relieve himself and thought: I still haven't told him the truth. He wasn't Jewish, not even half. He and Hermine had divorced because he squandered his entire inheritance on speculations. But even if I tell him that, he thought, it still wouldn't be the entire truth.

The river had changed names again, like a woman who keeps remarrying, and was now called the Merwede. Just before its confluence with the Maas and the Noord, Konrad brought the raft close to the bank so that Julius could jump ashore with a rope in his hand.

I've rafted pretty much the entire river, Konrad thought, from Wallreuth to Holland. My adventure is almost over.

They had just about reached the jetty, and the current was strong. Julius would have to weave among lampposts and parked automobiles, alternately tightening and slackening the rope. He turned up his collar and hung the coiled rope over his elbow.

Onlookers gathered on the quay; it had been years since they'd seen rafters at work here. A youth in a corduroy coat and cap jumped from his bicycle and gestured for them to throw him the rope. The water in the harbor was carpeted with duckweed and debris. A police car drove up; officers got out and took in the scene. The boy removed his cap, he was very light blond, and he waved it and gestured that he would pull in the raft. A policeman cupped his hands around his mouth and asked to see their permit.

"Julius!"

Julius straightened his gold-rimmed glasses and looked up, and Konrad suddenly saw how old he had become.

"Let's keep going!"

Julius tipped his black hat in consent.

The raft drifted further along the current of the Oude Maas, leaving the bemused helpers behind on the quay.

"What's fifteen guilders?" Konrad said. "I want to reach the sea."

The current carried them further west, and Julius, who had been silent for some time, consulted his map.

"That church steeple over there, that should be Puttershoek."

"And after that?"

"There is no city after that."

It was not snowing, but it was colder than ever.

They opened their last swingtop bottle of beer. Jenever would have been better.

Did you see that boy with the corduroy jacket, on the bike? That's how I could start, thought Julius. And then Konrad would say, "The one with the cap, you mean, in Dordrecht?

Of course. Why?" And then I would say: "I can't stop thinking about him. Konrad, the truth is, I'm not attracted to women. That's why Hermine divorced me. I couldn't perform my duties as a husband."

And then instead of speaking, Konrad would think back on the night when Julius returned from his failed adventure with Thekla von Wiedenhausen.

"Didn't you ever suspect anything?" would be Julius's next question.

He was fairly sure Konrad would answer no.

But say Konrad were to add, "You were plenty excited in that brothel in Koblenz."

Then it would be the moment to confess: "It wasn't because of Evchen. It was because of the Senegalese fellow. And because of you."

"I have to tell you something," Konrad said, holding up the beer bottle to be sure he didn't shortchange Julius before taking his last swig. "I have no imagination. You do. Rafting down this river was the only idea I've ever had. I'll go back to Wallreuth now, and once I'm home I'll fix up my mother's house. You'll go to America."

"Yeah," Julius mumbled and took the tin cigarette case from his coat pocket. "And set up a business in car tires and be a millionaire before you know it."

It was already getting dark when the river curved to the north and five tall flames appeared in the sky.

"What's that?" Konrad asked, excited and uneasy at the same time. The river was becoming stranger and stranger. He felt like he was in a Jules Verne story, where the heroes witnessed things they couldn't explain until the scientist traveling with them spelled it all out.

"Oil refineries at the Vondelingenplaat. They burn off methane gas."

"Without you I'd have never learned a thing," Konrad said. After a pause he added, "Without you I'd have never rafted all the way down this river."

"It's been a long voyage," Julius mumbled as they passed the lights of Delfshaven. It started snowing again, and they halfway covered themselves under a tarpaulin.

Konrad pointed to a large white sign on the shore with the number 17 on it.

"What does that mean?"

"Seventeen kilometers past Rotterdam, I think. This is the Nieuwe Waterweg."

Not much of a name, Julius thought, but it's still the same river. We were boys on the creek, youths on the Main, men on the Rhine. I loved him, I betrayed him, my whole life revolved around him. But we've never been closer than we are now, and in a few hours we'll reach the sea together as old men, without knowing each other. And we've essentially stolen this raft.

An enormous passenger ship with a thousand illuminated portholes charged past them on its way to sea and forced the raft to the edge of the canal. After Konrad had held them off the cement bank, he resumed his place next to Julius on the crate.

Julius took the tin case out of his pocket and offered him a flat cigarette.

"Do you know what love is?" Julius asked after they had lit their cigarettes.

"No," Konrad said, "I don't. I've never loved anyone. Not even myself. You're more worldly than I am."

"But surely you . . ."

"Once, with a pharmacist's widow in Nierst. But it didn't do anything for me. It was like I wasn't even there."

"You were in Egypt, sir, and did not see the pyramids?"

"How do you mean?"

"Sorry. Just a quote."

"All I've ever read were six books by Jules Verne," Konrad said as he stood up to unravel the system of range lights, beacons, and buoys on this busy stretch of river.

The last day of their journey began. Behind them, the clouds in the east resembled pennons that had caught fire in the rising sun.

The raft floated steadily downstream, rotating slowly toward the sea. They sat back-to-back on the crate, the pike raised like a mast without sails, and saw daybreak, the lightless west, and all points of the compass repeatedly pass by; reaped-clean beet fields, streets, quays, cranes, and factories, a maelstrom of loveless land.

"D'you think there'll be surf?" Konrad asked.

"I suppose so."

"I'm finally going to see the sea!"

"It won't be long now," Julius replied, "but don't get your hopes up."

Pierre and Adèle

He shall be purified by

Fire, Water, Air, and Earth

The deer stumbled after the reverberation from the shot had already died away, as though it only then realized it had been hit. Its forelegs buckled, and it slid, kneeling, in the direction of the river, its head held high. It was seized by the kind of panic that can also strike a human when he realizes something terrible has happened to him but doesn't yet know what. Lurching on its three good legs, it tried to reach the far side of the vale.

Two men—one young, one old—appeared from the bushes, their shotguns raised. Their hunting dog set off in yelping pursuit.

The deer, a young doe, plunged into the creek and waded through it with short, crooked leaps; her head, with rolling eyes and dripping chin, just above the surface.

Two other men appeared from the woods on the opposite side.

They, too, had their rifles at the ready, but rather than being aimed at the deer, they were pointed at the men across from them.

"Not one more step!" bellowed one of them. "Keep off our land!"

The deer staggered up the muddy bank toward the inevitable, sagged to the ground, and lay prone on the grass, its long neck bent backward.

The first pair of hunters approached. The eldest, who walked with difficulty, broke open his shotgun and draped it over his bent arm, the barrel pointing downward; at the same time, with his right hand, he felt in the pocket of his corduroy coat and slipped two new shells into the barrels.

"Listen, man," he shouted hoarsely. "Be reasonable. We shot her on our property. She's only five meters from us. It's our kill."

"Not a chance. She's on our land. Everything on this side of the boundary is ours."

As though to accentuate those words, his companion lowered the muzzle of his shotgun and, hardly taking his eyes off the men across from him, shot the deer in the head.

Her legs stretched for a brief moment, as though she considered a last-ditch flight and then gave in.

The dead, clouded-over doe eye still reflected two wooded riverbanks and four men. What it no longer saw was the dog, which, yapping with enthusiasm, had swum across the river and pounced upon her body.

"Call off that damn dog," said the one who had fired the coup de grace, "or he'll be next."

"Babouche, *ici*!" shouted one of the hunters.

The dog wagged its wet, furry tail in acknowledgement of the command, but at the same time it sank its teeth into the dead animal's soft underbelly.

"*Ici*, Babouche! *Viens!*"

"Call him off, or I'll blow him away," the man repeated, leveling his rifle. "It's my right. He's poaching."

"Don't you dare, you swine!" the older hunter threatened. "Babouche, heel!"

The dog, torn between duty and bloodlust, pulled a strand of gut from the deer's torn-open belly and backed through the mud and into the water, its ears pitched backward to hear its master's voice, its eyes glued on the enemy.

"Make him let go! I'll shoot!"

The younger hunter stepped into the creek, the water flowing above his rubber boots; he grabbed the dog by the collar and dragged it onto the shore.

The intestine now floated in the water like the loose end of an umbilical cord.

The shooter placed his foot on the deer, and one last puff of air escaped from the cadaver's belly.

The hunters kicked their dog, who had no idea what it had done wrong.

"You know this means war, don't you, bastard?"

"It's been war since your ancestors turned heretics. They should have wiped you all out. You've got no business in France."

"I'm warning you, you dirty collaborator. Set one foot on our side of the creek, and we shoot. I don't care if it's your dog or your daughter."

"Pathetic old cripple. Come on, let's get this game of ours home."

They lugged the deer by its legs up the bank, rifles clamped under their free arms, while the other hunters retreated into the woods on their side of the vale, dragging their befuddled dog with them.

High above their heads, three Mirages, the French air force's new supersonic jet fighters, tore past.

The vale was many miles long, but narrow. The meadowlands between either shore of the creek and the edge of the woods were at most a hundred meters wide, except at the spot where ruins from the Merovingian era, at one time a shrine devoted to Saint Godeberta, stood—more than this, no one knew. It was a favorite climbing place for goats.

The land to the right of the creek belonged to the Chrétiens, that to the left to the family Corbé; it had never been otherwise. The families hated each other, and this, too, had never been otherwise.

The Corbés were Huguenots, the Chrétiens Catholic. Since the Revolution, their farmsteads had been situated in different *départements*, so the only thing that bound them was the shared ownership of that narrow, uninhabited valley where in the summertime their livestock grazed.

Because the creek was slender and shallow in the summer, the animals would cross over, and trying to keep them separated was a fool's errand. This show of free will, however, did not tally with the two families' worldview. No Corbé in his right mind would accept a calf from a Catholic steer; no Chrétien could abide a heretic billy goat mounting their nannies.

To this end, they agreed to let their cattle or their goats and sheep graze in the valley on alternate years. This only led to more bad blood, because deep down, both parties were convinced that the other benefited unduly. The Chrétiens' heifers trampled the grass in a year that the Corbés only kept sheep; the Corbés' herds of cattle, claimed the Chrétiens, were far too large and displaced their goats.

But the main bone of contention was that the creek bed was constantly shifting, eroding the loam in the outside bends, taking land away from the one side and giving it to the other. By and large, this injustice was compensated in subsequent years by new, opposing meanders, and as seen over the centuries, neither the one family nor the other was ultimately disadvantaged—but from generation to generation, the Corbés as well as the Chrétiens were convinced that nature had systematically dealt them a bad hand.

The vale remained what it always had been, with its strips of grassland between the wooded hillsides, and the winding silver ribbon of the Issou more or less in the middle.

Pierre Corbé was seven and was standing in the creek with his pant legs rolled up, netting for sticklebacks. His four-year-old brother had dozed off in the grass, a still-damp net over his face to keep away the hornets.

Pierre already had a dozen of the tiny fish in his jam jar.

The Chrétien girls walked on the far bank. They had straw hats and pretended to pick berries at the edge of the woods, but of course the berries weren't ripe yet at this time of year. They all wore white linen dresses, and the oldest sister was at least thirteen. They were only here to spoil their fun. It's not fair when you're the oldest and only seven and your little brother is just a tyke, and they show up with a whole gang and their leader is almost a grown-up and they're all girls. Even the youngest was older than him. That was because, according to his father, Catholics bred like rabbits.

He had just scooped out a nice one that had been chasing a water flea, and he tipped it into his jam pot when the Chrétien girls approached him, like a swarm of white vultures.

He tried in vain to pull up his little brother in time.

"Hey, you there," a voice resounded through the valley, "what are you doing there? You can't go in our creek."

"Your creek?" he called back. "It's not your creek. The creek is the boundary, and a boundary is everybody's."

"Oh really? Is that what Mr. Calvin says? Well, my father says that the creek is the boundary, and you people have no business coming on our side."

"I wasn't on your side. I was standing in the middle of the creek."

"Is that so? And whose is the middle? Yours, you reckon? The middle is nobody's."

"He just pinched a stickleback from our side," said one of the younger sisters. "I saw it myself."

"You can't fish in our water," the leader said, wading in up to her calves. "Give it here, that jam pot."

"No, I won't," Pierre said defiantly. "Fish swim wherever they want, and I do what I want too. That's none of Rome's business."

"All right, then," she said, "we'll fight it out. Put 'em up, if you dare."

"I don't fight with girls."

"Because you're a sissy!"

"You're way bigger and there are five of you and I have to look after my kid brother, that's why."

"If you don't dare, I'll come over there and dump your sticklebacks into the creek."

While Pierre pulled his brother upright, the girls began to jeer and throw clumps of mud and hunks of chalk at him.

"Heretic! Heretic!" shrieked one of the younger sisters, and she tried to fling a cow patty at them with a stick. The girls had the upper hand. They held on to their straw hats, insofar as they hadn't fallen to the grass already, and bombarded him with anything within reach. And they had on those white dresses, while all the mothers, aunts, sisters, and girl cousins in his family wore dark clothing. It did make them look pretty, he thought, until a stone knocked over his jam jar. He tried to scoop up the wriggling sticklebacks, but it was as if they did not want to be rescued.

Just then, a distant buzz caught their attention. It was a sound the children had never heard before. It came from the sky.

The boys stood up, clutching their nets; the girls ceased their assault and shielded their eyes with their hands.

To the west, between the white clouds and the treetops, something no one had ever heard or seen before approached.

It was a flying machine.

At a spot in the world where only falcons or crows flew was the outline of a man-made thing that cut through the azure Breton sky as though it had only just now been discovered.

The machine was two-tiered, and because of its vertical partitions and cube-like tail, it most resembled a crate or a flying stall. But it was operated by a clearly visible hero wearing a leather cap. Moreover, he seemed to be waving to them.

It dipped above the valley and, rocking on the gentle westerly wind, headed toward Nantes.

"Santos-Dumont!" Pierre screamed, running after it.

"Who?" the eldest girl called out.

"Santos-Dumont!" Pierre cried. "The aviator! He's from Brazil!"

Shouting and waving, the children all chased after the airplane, trying to keep up with its shadow as it glided over the creek and vale.

"Santos-Dumont!" they cheered as though they had found a mutual idol, and they ran after it and waved for their lives, each on their own side of the creek.

It was paradoxical but not illogical that the families had turned to a Jewish mediator to settle their dispute.

Eduard Solomon was a third-generation solicitor practicing in Lorient, a calm, well-spoken young man who read modern authors like Claudel and Romains. The ongoing case of Chrétien versus Corbé represented a considerable source of income for his family, and partly for that reason, his father, retired but still busying himself with the firm's day-to-day matters, was hardly keen to reach a definitive settlement.

"Supposing those obstinate farmers agree—what good is that to *us*? Let them go on arguing and come to us year after year for mediation . . . In an ideal world, there would be no place for people like us anymore."

"Which do you mean, us Jews or us lawyers?"

"Us lawyers—and mind your tone, Eduard. Everything you are and have is thanks to me."

"I know that, Father. I beg your pardon. Another glass of Calvados?"

Eduard refilled the glasses on the folding table.

There was a stiff breeze; between the steep coast on which their villa stood and the Île de Groix, the gray-green sea showed a pattern of frothy stripes.

Both men were dressed in black, as behooved their status: the father in old-fashioned tails with a brocade vest, the son in a sober three-piece suit with narrow lapels.

"This villa—which you will inherit—I built. I paid your tuition to law school. Our firm's profits increase by the year. And you have nothing better to do than better the world?"

"Why shouldn't I better the world, if I can?" Eduard asked.

"Because you can't," his father said, pursing his thick, pale-pink lips over the rim of his liqueur glass. "And because it would not be in our best interest." He wiped off his moustache and stroked his beard.

"You wouldn't want a perfect world, Father?" Eduard asked, smiling.

"No. First of all"—his father counted off on his fingers—"because this is my world, and I don't like it when someone just goes and changes it. Second, because it would jeopardize the labor market. In a perfect world, there would be no need for doctors, because no one would get sick; nor for judges, lawyers, or gendarmes; nor for soldiers or solicitors. And furthermore, is a perfect world what God wants for us?"

"You've even got a theological argument?"

"To the woman He said: 'In pain you will bring forth children.' And to the man He said: 'By the sweat of your face you will eat bread.'"

Eduard shook his head and got up to move the potted oleander out of the wind.

"Even so, I'd like to show you the proposals I plan to present to the families."

"I'd prefer Camembert with olives."

"I've drawn them in on maps of the valley."

"My own father showed me maps like these, once. Nothing ever came of it."

"I'd appreciate your opinion before I go talk to the Chrétiens and the Corbés."

"Go on, then. Bring something to weigh them down. And, if you please, some Camembert and olives."

A large chasse-marée with dark-red sails turned into the wind toward the jetty. The elder Solomon could predict precisely when it would tack.

Eduard unfolded three maps, weighing them down with a bottle of wine, a carafe of water, a plate of cheese and olives, and a marble ashtray.

Before he could say anything, as his mouth was full, his father began wagging his index finger impatiently here and there above the first map, on which a horizontal equator drawn in purple pencil separated the area into a northern and a southern half.

"Already suggested this once," he said as he broke off a piece of bread. "A lost cause. The southern part of the valley is a bit wider . . ."

"I've adjusted it for that."

"And besides, neither family would put it past the other one to pollute or poison the river upstream if they were to opt for the southern half."

"And this one?"

"I don't see anything. What's your point?"

Eduard indicated a slip of paper with text written in his own calligraphic hand and attached to the map, explaining how the families would grant each other alternate use of the entire valley for a period of twelve years.

"That's creative, I'll admit . . . I believe there's something like it in Leviticus. But I'm telling you, they'll never go along with it. The Chrétiens might be able to afford it, but the Corbés can't survive for twelve years without that income. Besides, they'd probably chop down all the trees in their last year. Or the other party would suspect them of doing so. No contract is any match for these people. Twelve years on, it will be all-out war. Or just one year on, should you think of suggesting a shorter term."

Eduard sighed and picked up the carafe to pour himself a glass. The third map fluttered up and stuck against his chest like a paper toga.

"The point is, any solution that requires one of the families to relinquish part of their land or any of their rights doesn't stand a chance. Ergo, there will never be a solution. What've you got on that third map?"

"I give up for today. Time for a glass of wine. Supper is almost ready."

The chasse-marée lowered its gaff sails, leaving only the triangular jib visible above the pier.

"Come, let's have a look, as long as we're at it," his father said. "Then we'll be done with it."

With something close to aversion, Eduard peeled the map from his chest and spread it out on the table. There was a red line straight down the length of the vale.

"Aha, the classic solution: a fence down the middle. The creek meanders to the right or to the left, but the line of demarcation stays the same. A topographic solution entirely in the spirit of the Enlightenment. I can tell you a good story about that."

"I'm listening," Eduard said, as he poured two glasses of Bordeaux.

"In the year 1851, when I was a young law student myself, my father attempted the same thing. It was the most progress we had ever made in the case. The families had even agreed to split the cost of the surveyor and the placement of the fence. But . . ."

"One family pulled out at the last minute?"

"No—high water. The valley was inundated all the way to the woods' edge. All the better, my father said: this surveyor can do his work and drive the stakes from a rowboat. What more objective way to draw a boundary, when you can't see the land?"

"Perfect! What went wrong?"

"Nothing, at least with the surveying. The valley had turned into a lake. An elegant, nearly endless row of stakes ran straight through it, from the headwaters down to where the property ended. But when the water receded, they discovered that the creek bed had shifted, making a huge bend to the west, thus giving the Chrétiens some six hundred square meters of mud. So of course they vetoed the new demarcation line."

"And everything stayed as it was. My God, those people are shortsighted."

"That's just how it is. A few years later, incidentally, there was more land on the Corbés' side. The truth is, they don't want a solution."

Eduard folded up the maps, made a little brick-sized stack of them, and lined up their edges with his fingertips. He tied them up with a black ribbon, like a widower might with letters to his wife.

The elder Solomon watched him sardonically and sipped his Bordeaux.

"I'll archive this," Eduard said, "but I still hope to come up with a solution one day, something they simply can't refuse, to get this thing settled once and for all."

"Pipe dreams, my boy," said his father. "Our name might be Solomon—but in this case, wisdom just isn't enough."

After the Great War, too, a resolution seemed more elusive than ever. When Pierre Corbé, who had been called up in the final year and had been interned as a German prisoner of war, returned and took over the farm, Adèle Chrétien, who had no brothers, had married Corentin Berthou, the son of one of Brittany's largest landowners, and who defended the interests of the family with merciless fanaticism, and a new confrontation loomed.

Eduard, by now a heavyset man who read Gide and Mauriac, took the train one Sunday afternoon to the local station at Auray and wandered through the valley, so as to assess the situation.

Although he did not frequent the great outdoors, he gradually began to enjoy the undertaking. It was a fine spring day, and the meandering creek glistened between the green grasslands, which, as his map showed, were everywhere nearly equally wide. Having traversed a number of kilometers, he decided to rest and found a suitable spot: the gray stones upon a hillock, which were said to be the ruins of a chapel devoted to Saint Godeberta. He shared the spot with a few goats.

This year they would be Corbé's, he thought, although he couldn't say for sure. A large billy goat lay on the highest stone and had no plans to vacate it. Eduard sat down on a lower one, from which he still had a view of the entire valley. The goat eyed him, one skinny foreleg with a cloven hoof dangling over the edge, the other folded sideways under his body. His bloated, hirsute belly rested on the warm stone and made the occasional muscular contraction. Flies buzzed.

Now this is nature, he thought, the real thing in the midst of our civilized France. This hillock could just as well be a prehistoric tumulus. Just then, the church bells of Auray chimed. The steeple was hidden behind the wooded hills. It was a reassuring thought that the Chrétiens were now at Mass, and Pierre Corbé would be at a service at the distant Protestant church in Camors. He had the place to himself. He took a sandwich from his tin lunch box, uncorked the bottle of cider he brought with him, and opened his portfolio.

There, before him, lay the problem.

The creek had split.

At the broadest part of the valley, the creek had branched into two, to all appearances, equally wide halves, forming a long elliptical island in the middle before rejoining further up. His father and grandfather never had to deal with this. Which branch was the boundary?

The goats, who by now had all closed in around him, had other matters in mind and sidled ever closer to his lunch box. His attempts to shoo them off had no effect whatsoever.

The divided course of the creek would require negotiations, and negotiating with the Corbés and the Chrétiens was well-nigh impossible. A good, heavy rainfall for a few weeks, which might cause the stream to shift its bed yet again, could solve the problem, but such an occurrence transpiring this year was doubtful. In the meantime, something had to happen, of this he was certain.

A brown goat with a black dorsal stripe had planted her forelegs between his thighs and looked him straight in the eye. Eduard was fairly sure goats didn't attack humans, but all the same, he wasn't entirely at ease. He threw the crust from his bread as far as he could, just to have some peace.

While thumbing through his portfolio, a yellowed newspaper clipping from the *l'Ouest-Éclair* fell out into his hands. Pierre Corbé's great-grandfather and Adèle Chrétien's grandfather had been found dead on the nearly dried-up riverbed. Corbé's head had been bashed in, and Chrétien had taken a bullet through the heart.

There were no witnesses, and no one had any clue as to the circumstances, but public opinion in Catholic Brittany was that Chrétien had been cravenly shot dead and with his last bit of strength had brained his murderer.

The opposing party's lawyer argued, on the contrary, that the victim, the elderly Corbé, had laid his hunting rifle on the riverbank and was constructing a small stone dam so as to sluice water to his thirsty cattle, when Chrétien took his own rifle by the barrel and struck the defenseless old man with its butt, inadvertently firing the avenging shot upon himself, ". . . and was felled by the same sanguineous act that took the life of his victim . . . Or, perhaps, by the hand of God."

According to the court in Rennes, however, Corbé's weapon had also been fired.

The date, written in nearly faded ink on the upper corner of the article, read 17 August 1852.

My God, Eduard thought to himself. Here we are in the twentieth century, a peace treaty is being drawn up in Versailles to forestall future wars once and for all, and these families persist in passing their petty feud from father to son. The sleep of reason produces monsters. There had to be a solution. He tucked away the clipping and gazed out over the ostensibly tranquil valley, following the branched and reunited waterway with his eyes. If both parties felt shortchanged, then . . . It was such a bold idea that he hardly dared to imagine it to its conclusion and allowed himself to be distracted by a pair of falcons, gliding around each other in a double helix, scouring the ground for prey.

By now it had become quite hot, and the buzz of the flies ever more intrusive. He unbuttoned his collar and vest. He became more aware of the stench of the goat droppings among the stones of the ruins. Maybe not the best place for a picnic after all. Again he let his gaze follow the glistening creek, until in the distance it vanished behind a bend in the valley. One could—

Something tugged at his hat.

The buck was now standing directly behind him, its silhouette standing out against the blue sky. His horns and beard made his head look four times longer than it really was. He curled his upper lip and licked his snout with his long tongue, staring at Eduard with tiny pupils. An impressive mask, Eduard thought. Beelzebub, the lord of the flies. Strange to think that goats were content to eat grass; they looked to him like carnivores. He gathered up his portfolio and lunch box and prepared to leave. He had seen enough.

As he descended the hillock, a long row of cows appeared across the river. If these were Corbé's goats, then those must be the Chrétiens' cows.

He began the trek back to the Auray train station. The cows appeared to have nothing better to do than follow him in single file. The appearance of a human being in this remote valley was probably something quite special and carried with it certain expectations, which, however, he was unable to satisfy.

Eduard stopped and explained to them that he could do nothing for them, that he could not milk them and was not a cattleman. The frontmost cow listened attentively, but as soon as he continued walking, she did the same. It was some time before she stayed put, swishing her tail to brush the flies off her rump—a disciple who eventually lost faith.

This is not my world, Eduard thought, and as he walked, he began pondering the proposal details he planned to work out at home.

But he had underestimated the exceptional instinct that every farmer possesses when someone is on his land, even if it's a Sunday; a man on horseback came galloping at him.

It was Corentin Berthou.

Even without much equestrian knowledge, Eduard could see that Berthou was a poor horseman. He sat upright in his saddle, with short stirrups, and with every bounce he slapped his sorrel's flank with his crop.

Seeing as there was no escape, Eduard stopped and removed his hat. Corentin brought his horse to a halt and greeted him by sliding his cap back slightly with the tip of his whip.

"Bonjour, maître."

"Bonjour, Monsieur Berthou. I've been having a stroll."

"Always welcome, maître," Corentin said, and jovially slapped his horse's neck. The animal responded with an indifferent swivel of the ears. "You've seen the site of our new barn, I take it? We'll be laying the foundation tomorrow."

"Where, exactly?" Eduard asked warily.

"Just on the shore, on our side of the river."

"On the new island."

"Indeed," Corentin grinned.

The Corbés had a dark complexion and were smallish people with unpronounced but regular features; the Chrétiens were in general taller, tended to be blond, and often had large noses, ears, and chins. But the new man did not resemble them in the slightest. He was pale and freckled, with cropped reddish hair.

"Pierre Corbé won't stand for that. He has as much right to this new, temporary island as you do."

"And what can he do about it—take me to court? If I'm not mistaken, he's nearly broke. But as a solicitor you'll know more than I do, I expect?"

"I'm not at liberty to discuss it, Monsieur Berthou."

"You're not, are you? As you wish. But I do hope you realize who the future belongs to and that you'll take appropriate measures. It's said that your sort have a nose for that."

"You're referring to the fact that I'm Jewish?"

"I didn't want to put it that explicitly, maître. I'm not biased myself, as long as every man knows his place."

Eduard pulled himself together, and placed a hand on the horse's bridle. "Don't do it, Monsieur Berthou. The law is not on your side."

"Oh really? On whose side is it, then? The Corbés fight with every means they have, and for centuries they've profited from every new bend in the river. I've read the deeds. And they murdered my wife's grandfather."

"That has never been proved. And besides—where does the river flow? Look over your shoulder."

"I don't need to look. I know this river."

"It flows through the middle of the valley, Monsieur Berthou, where it always has done. It cannot do otherwise; it is a fact of nature. A river does just not meander up a hillside, to do one landowner or the other a favor. It flows where it has always flowed, with minimal deviations where the bed is flat. The river is the boundary. Do respect it."

"I respect nothing that puts my family at a disadvantage. You simply don't think like a landowner, Maître Solomon. How could you? You come from different stock."

The sorrel snorted, and he quickly let go of the reins. Corentin laughed, and tugged fiercely on the double bridle until his horse stood still, its neck doubled forward and its chest splotched with froth.

"Don't do it," Eduard repeated. "I have a proposal, that perhaps might—"

"Have a pleasant walk, maître. You know the way to the station?" He turned his horse and galloped back toward the island.

The barn was never built, because the cartload of stones Berthou had brought to the island soon lay on Corbé's side of the river. It was a dry May, and the river abandoned its overconfident branching efforts and was satisfied to settle back into its old bed.

Nor did Eduard ever get the chance to present his proposal: Pierre Corbé loaded the stones onto a wagon and brought them to his farm without granting Berthou, who stood ranting across the river, so much as a glance. He would never forgive this attempt at land theft. Just as the Chrétiens would never forgive the pilfering of their stones. From that day onward, both parties refused any form of consultation.

When Adèle sat at the mirror, she never actually looked at herself. She was well aware of her appearance and had no desire to reacquaint herself with it. She would fix her glance on the reflection of her earlobe while attaching a pearl to it, on the column of her neck while clasping her triple-strand coral necklace, on her dark-blond braids while winding them around her head. But she did not look at herself. Not that she had any reason to doubt her appearance: she was the model of a stately Breton woman in the prime of her life. Her imperturbable eyes seemed made to take on the entire world.

But she avoided her reflection because she did not want to see what her husband desired. She felt nothing but revulsion for Corentin. When her father died, she, the heiress, was seen as a fine match, and everyone urged her to accept Berthou's advances because his family was powerful and would protect her against the Corbés.

Her husband was libidinous, but no children were born.

Adèle had nothing more in common with the young woman who had entered into that marriage, but time had been merciless, for she was still as beautiful as the bride she now so despised.

She had not exchanged a word with Pierre Corbé since the day they argued by the water, back when they were children. She sometimes saw him in the distance: a stocky, dark-haired man who performed his labors and attended to his business with an uncompromising humility that exuded a kind of strength. He had been decorated at the front, she knew, while Corentin had been a dealer of Renault automobiles. Corentin also drank, abused animals, was an anti-Semite, and was incapable, she now knew, of any emotions other than conceit and self-pity. And her husband did not listen to her. Building a barn on that temporary island was a stupid idea, but she could not talk him out of it. That was not how you played the game. It only ended in humiliation, just as she had predicted.

Pierre Corbé had undertaken numerous attempts to marry. Pickings were slim in the small Protestant community, and there was no girl among them he could imagine as his wife. So he took the laborious path of placing anonymous personal advertisements in various provincial newspapers, even as far afield as Normandy and Charente. A period of wearisome correspondence led to all of two meetings. For the first, he had to take the train to Caen. The woman turned out, for starters, to be twenty years older than he had presumed and was a religious lunatic to boot. The second candidate was a bubbly grocer's daughter with bulges and curves in unusual places and who soon confessed not to be Protestant at all, but from Catholic folk, although, she assured him, it did not matter to her a whit. Pierre remained a bachelor. At least the farmstead would stay in the family after his death, because even though his younger brother had died, there were still a few Corbés in Brittany. That he hardly knew them personally was of no consequence.

His life had narrowed to carrying out his duties, or whatever he regarded as such. Six days thou shalt work. Happiness did not figure into it.

When Pierre Corbé looked in the mirror, it was to shave or if he contemplated a visit to the dentist. He took his looks as a given. Vanity was a torment of the soul. Of course he could recognize himself in a group photo of his battalion—if nothing else because of the scar on his upper lip—just as one picks out one's coat and hat from a cloakroom, but his appearance did not concern him in the least.

He had no other notion of self than his role in the order of things, as the Bible had taught him. What counted in the world were money and power, and of these he had precious little. And land. Land was everything.

For him, Adèle Chrétien was like the queens from the olden days, whom he had read about at school: she had allied herself with a powerful suitor in order to keep her realm. Corentin Berthou was a punishment of the Lord. It was as though the Almighty, who had once spread plagues across heathen Egypt, was out to test his faith by presenting him with a new enemy.

There was one memory that went further back than the day they argued at the creek, although Pierre thought he might be remembering something he had only dreamed.

He and Adèle were both still small, and they stood on either side of the creek, which in the dream was tiny and twinkling.

"If you jump, I will!" shouted Adèle, who was wearing a little straw hat. Her face was smeared with blueberry juice.

"No, you can't!" Pierre called back. "This is our side."

"I know. And this side is ours. But if we both jump at the same time . . . then, just for second, your side is mine, and mine is yours!"

"What do you mean? If my father catches us, I'll get a thrashing."

"Well, if we're both in the air at the same time, and then I'm on your side and you're on mine, then it's like we just trade land for a minute, right?"

She took a few steps back to get a running start, swishing her dress ostentatiously from side to side, as though she were capable of taking an enormous leap.

"Just once, then," Pierre called back.

"Fraidy-cat!" Adèle shouted.

They sailed alongside each other and landed on opposite banks.

"Corbé, Corbé!" she cheered, dancing in a circle. "I'm on Corbés' land!"

"Chrétien, Chrétien!" Pierre hollered, and made odd somersaults.

"One more time!" Adèle exclaimed, and once again they jumped simultaneously over the water.

"And again, hooray, hooray!"

In his dream, they finally flopped, exhausted, in the grass on their own side of the river. Adèle rubbed her skinny knees, and he rolled onto his back and let out a fart.

"You see? It works if we both jump at the same time," Adèle panted. "Tomorrow too?"

"Maybe," he replied.

And Adèle, for her part, thought she recalled that they did do it again, but she wasn't entirely sure.

In the year the French occupied the shores of the Rhine, an incident occurred that would leave Pierre an invalid; thereafter he could walk only with the aid of a prosthetic leg.

The day had already started strangely. The Chrétiens' livestock was nowhere to be seen. It was hot and still, and the cloudless sky seemed two-dimensional: a flat blue surface behind the static green of the hillsides. Pierre had counted his heifers and was preparing to return home for his midday meal when he spotted the lapwings. The female dragged herself with exaggerated drama away from him through the reeds, pretending she had a broken wing. Pierre walked back and forth along the shore and from her behavior guessed that the nest must be on the other side of the creek.

He glanced up and down the vale. There was no one in sight.

The temptation was too great. He was a law-abiding man, if only to keep his conscience pure for the Lord, but helping himself to a few lapwing eggs was really quite innocent. He'd done so since he was a boy.

The creek was at most knee-deep at this spot, and there wasn't a soul in sight.

He removed his shoes and socks, rolled up his trouser legs. The lapwing performed a heartrendingly dramatic solo on the riverbank. Pierre chuckled and waded into the cool water, keeping one eye on the treacherous bottom and the other on the spot where he suspected he'd find the nest.

There it was, no more than ten meters from the shoreline.

Four spotted eggs.

He reached out his hand and took one more step, and then the fox trap snapped shut.

He registered the dull clunk and looked down. The large, toothed jaws had clamped shut just above his ankle.

He stood up to check whether there were any witnesses; there were none. Only then came the pain, strange and overwhelming. The scream with which he collapsed before losing consciousness was mostly one of surprise.

Upon reopening his eyes, the first thing he saw were the four spotted eggs in the shallow nest, almost within reach, and after that, the monstrous jaws of the trap that held him captive.

It was not your normal fox trap. It was a vintage exemplar that in his grandfather's day had been used to catch roving wolves. It would have snapped a fox paw straight through. The serrated jaws nearly met, deep in his leg.

Stupid of me, he thought, and lifted the chain to see where it led. To a long, wrought-iron peg hammered deep into the clay.

Pierre needed time, and lay down on his back, assailed by the lapwing parents who returned to claim their unhatched brood.

Heavy raindrops began falling on his face and hands. Light flashed beyond the wispy clouds. Pierre saw short zigzags of lightning and for a moment wondered if this was perhaps the veins bursting in his eyeballs. The pain was intense.

A heavy downpour pummeled him even deeper into the grass. Something had to be done.

He sat up and attempted the most obvious: to open the trap. But it would not budge. Hand over hand, he pulled himself by the chain toward the peg. Standing on one leg, he tugged it out of the clay. He dragged himself, clutching the peg and clamp, back to the river and waded through it on his hands and knees. Now he was at least on his own property.

The thunderstorm broke in a fury; the two little black lapwing crests poked out stoically from their nest above the rain-battered grass.

He took his walking stick and, using it as a lever, managed to pry open the clamp. This brought with it another, new pain, somehow more excruciating than before.

Pierre wiped the rain from his eyes and looked at the gaping wound and the tattered stocking of streaming blood.

So that's why there was no livestock on the other side. Berthou had caught him out, but he'd be damned if he would give him the satisfaction of this triumph.

He got up and flung the trap—chain, peg and all—to the other side of the river.

He hung his shoes around his neck and staggered up the bank to the woods. But once he had reached safety and looked back, he realized that this would not do. Berthou would find the sprung trap and the loose chain, and as soon as he saw Pierre limp, he would put two and two together.

He found a branch that could serve as a crutch, and dragged himself back to the water's edge.

The pouring rain obscured the vale almost completely. Forked lightning bolts lit up the firmament. He resembled a sinner from the grotesque world of Gustave Doré, returning to the scene of a calamity to wipe out the tracks of a crime of which he himself was the victim.

Now the thunderclouds discharged their load directly above him. He waded back across the river, leaning on his forked branch; he picked up the hefty trap and brought it to the lapwing nest. He pried the toothed maw open just enough to wedge a stone in between the jaws, eventually forcing the coil springs far enough open to reset the cruel instrument.

The lapwings sat in motionless fatalism on their eggs.

He crawled through the grass, located the hole where the peg had been, and used the stone to hammer it back into the ground.

Now everything was as it had been.

Pierre dragged himself back across the river and up the bank to where he'd left his shoes. He moved slowly but deliberately and knew that despite the pain he would be able to reach his house. On one foot, and with the help of his makeshift crutch, he hobbled through the woods.

The rain let up, and a white mist rose skyward, like incense from an abandoned altar. It was still oppressively hot.

Corentin Berthou approached along the far side. Now and then he stopped to inspect a spot in the grass. The other fox traps, Pierre thought, he's laid out a whole row of them, just along the riverbank. Then he bent over and picked up what were surely lapwing eggs and carefully placed them in the pocket of his wide-cut coat. Never before had Pierre hated anyone as much as he did Corentin Berthou at that moment.

At home, he swathed his leg and lay down on his bed. He did not want to call a doctor. On the fourth day, his jaw, and then the rest of his body, started to stiffen. His face froze in a grimace of agony, and his back muscles were so completely cramped that his body was bent into a backward arch. It was tetanus.

He suffered more than he ever imagined being able to endure, but still he refused to call for a doctor. It was *his* pain.

It was retribution for his sins, and that was nobody's business but his own.

Besides, he did not trust the village doctor, who, after all, would offhandedly give him unasked-for updates on Adèle's childlessness. Never, never must Berthou find out that he had caught him out.

He survived, but his leg had to be amputated below the knee. Pierre never again participated in the *Quatorze-Juillet* parade. His peg leg was not worthy of admiration, like those of his war comrades.

The highlight of the liturgical calendar was the grand procession in Rennes during the Feast of the Sacred Heart, the third Friday after Pentecost.

Corentin and Adèle Berthou took part every year. He was one of the men who carried the Holy Madonna, and she joined other prominent women at the head of the procession, a palm frond in her hands.

It was the custom that effigies of the Virgin Mary would be brought to the city from the churches in the surrounding parishes and assembled at around noon on the Place Saint Etienne, where they were placed in a circle, on tables covered in richly embroidered velvet fabric; these were also carried from the individual villages, which was a laborious and thankless job for the men and boys lower down the social ladder. They gave the procession something clownish in the way they shuffled, the draperies obscuring much of their view, behind the Mother of God, like the back halves of devout donkeys.

The men fortified themselves with an aperitif at the cafés on the periphery of Place Saint Etienne, and the women sought the coolness of the benches and the edge of the fountain in the shadow of the sycamores.

Adèle accepted a glass of lemonade a girl brought her, and closed her eyes. She did not feel well, and the cathedral was still half an hour's walk through the crowded streets of Rennes; the band of her large lace cap dug into her forehead, and her stiff corset was so tight that she was unable to sweat out the heat. Just a few more hours and it would be over. She mustn't show any weakness; it was an honor to lead the procession.

She half opened her eyes, so as not to lose the world entirely, and the girl's dark skirt made way for a view of her husband, who stood outside Café Thiers, holding a glass of pastis.

Although his family came from Brest, he wore the traditional attire of her native region, with a wide-brimmed hat and a sash tied low on the hips. Anyone who saw his reddish-blond hair and perpetual smile would think him a man of the world, someone who knew how to get along with people. Only she knew his true colors, because she was married to him.

It vexed her that he did not seem to age. He was still slim. Life had left no traces on his face.

She desperately longed to finally become old and unattractive, and thus be spared his lust. But nature was slow to heed her wishes. She had put on some weight recently, her face was a bit rounder, but she was still very much the woman she no longer wished to be.

He still had her, if he wasn't too drunk, and took pleasure in telling her he did so only because it was his marital duty, that there were so many young girls he could have, but that this was part of the bargain, even if you only married for money.

Perhaps he couldn't do anything about it. That was the best thing she could say about him. And if you can't say anything good about your husband, you better not say anything at all. Ever.

Adèle absently swept the cobblestones between her feet with the palm frond, and looked back up.

The five Madonnas were gathered around her. They only saw one another once a year, at this spot across from Café Thiers. They gazed serenely, each in harmony with her own proportion, their holy heads standing out against the blue sky.

The Madonna of Rennes was immense and required eight bearers. She rose up from an artfully constructed decor of blue pleats spangled with countless stars, as stately and rigid as a long-reigning monarch.

It suddenly seemed to Adèle that the Madonnas were in conversation, as if on this day, once a year, they discussed the fortunes of the world, while the men who had borne them here, and would soon carry them to the cathedral, drank pastis.

What might they say to one another, that rustic wooden Madonna there and that absurdly tenderhearted one next to her, who had the misfortune to have been created by a lesser artist, and the white, neoclassical one from the basilica in Pacé, who always gave the impression of considering herself too good for this company, and her own dearest Mother of God, the pregnant one from the parish chapel of Noyal, who resembled a Breton peasant girl?

She heard a shout and saw men point up; Berthou came running from the café and now stood in the middle of the square with outstretched arms, pastis in hand, and cried out: "Vive la France."

Above the Madonnas, a large formation of bombers flew eastward, toward Germany, a spectacle they'd seen practically every day since Liberation. The airplanes passed at such a height that they were inaudible, making her husband's hollering all the more strident.

"*Allez, les Américains*! To Berlin! To Berlin!"

There was no telling if her husband, like old Louis Renault, would be accused of treason and arrested, for it was common knowledge that as a shareholder he had collaborated. It was a disgrace her family would never live down.

Never had she despised anything or anyone as much as this charlatan, who couldn't plow a straight furrow but posed as a gentleman farmer, who pretended to be a man but was nothing but a depraved little boy.

He had been of use to her in her struggle against the Corbés, but no woman should have to pay such a price, even for her worst transgressions.

"Let him die before me," she prayed to the stoic heads of the five Virgin Marys. She had missed her period for the first time ever, a few months in a row now, and perhaps she could look forward to a spell of peace. "Grant me old age without him," she prayed, "and I promise . . ."

All of a sudden it seemed—possibly because of the wispy white clouds passing behind her halo—as though the pregnant Madonna of Noyal leaned forward over her. Against the bright background, she was a black silhouette and looked like a leaning tree trunk that might fall over and crush her. Adèle closed her eyes to shut out the optical illusion, and felt herself become queasy.

She was forty-eight years old, and it could hardly be possible, but she knew that it was so.

She lay her hands on her belly, and her chin sank to her chest. "Help me," she whispered.

The girl who had brought the lemonade came back and bent over her, one hand on the plaster foot of the Madonna, who was dressed in the same costume as she.

"Can I do anything for you, madame?" she asked, concerned.

"No," Adèle replied curtly.

Berthou ambled back to the café, his index finger raised to lend credence to some loose prophecy. She saw how dismissive the other men reacted, but this was no comfort to her, not any longer.

The girl was named Marie-France, and before Berthou disappeared behind bars for high treason, he predicted that a woman who bore a child at such an abnormally advanced age would not glean much pleasure from it.

And all signs pointed to him being right. Marie-France had inherited his red hair and pale complexion, and was an unlovable child: weak, sickly, ungrateful.

Perhaps it was out of desperation that Adèle accepted Solomon's invitation, perhaps it was the need to defend her own interests, now that her husband was behind bars and deemed legally unfit. It could also be that, so much having gone wrong in her life, she was inclined to try something new in the hope that something good might come of it.

But curiosity also played a role: she had not seen Eduard Solomon since he'd fled to America at the outset of the war.

Why Pierre accepted the invitation, he didn't really know himself. He was hardly feeling conciliatory, now even less than ever. Nor was there anything noble about it—that his enemy now faced him herself, without her husband at her side, did not mollify him a bit. Maybe he hoped to finally stand face-to-face with this proud woman without her taking cover behind Berthou's clout. He felt stronger now that his adversary was named Chrétien, the way it had always been.

And there was another reason to accept the invitation: Eduard Solomon was a war hero who had landed on Utah Beach with the Second Division of the Free French Forces and had taken part in the liberation of Paris.

Pierre and Adèle sat across from each other at either end of the massive desk in the solicitor's office—the first time in half of a century that a Corbé and a Chrétien occupied the same space that was not a courtroom.

They avoided each other's glance until Eduard, seated between them at his desk, read out the various complaints and accusations from both sides, which they had drawn up at his request. He did this in a calm tone of voice, unemotionally, like a family doctor reading through an old dossier. The previous September there had been an incident whereby Corbé's goats were said to have gnawed the bark off some fruit trees the Chrétiens had planted in their meadow; earlier that summer, a Chrétien cow had died of colic, because Pierre Corbé had refused to let the veterinarian onto his land, etcetera.

Adèle and Pierre listened dispassionately to the reading and only shot a glance across the desk when they thought the other one wasn't looking.

He's a bitter old man, she thought to herself, who has to fend for himself entirely. A solitary bachelor, half-invalid, and poor. Scarred by that joyless religion of his. At least I have a child, even if it's only a daughter. And we're rich. Just imagine allowing an animal to die simply because you think you have the power to do so.

She's desperately unhappy, he thought to himself, despite that feigned dignity. Is she not ashamed, the wife of a traitor, to sit here and listen to Maître Solomon, a decorated war hero with the tricolor behind him and the Croix de Lorraine on his lapel, sum up her misdeeds? Plant fruit trees where you know they're bound to be gnawed on, only to claim damages after the fact. Devious papist ways.

Even without eye contact, each was so involved with the other that they only really started listening when Solomon got to the crux of the matter: his assessment that the bad blood between the two families boiled down to the fact that each felt disadvantaged by the varying course of the river, which first took land away from one party and then from the other. Was this correct?

Yes, Pierre said, since day one, the creek that marked the boundary ate into his land, and expanded that of the Chrétiens. This had specifically been the case in the years 1851, 1894, and 1919, and, to a lesser degree, more or less yearly.

Indeed, Adèle confirmed, the river, which formed the boundary, appeared to be biased. In 1816, 1862, 1921, and 1931, it gave nearly three quarters of the valley to the Corbés. And the aerial photographs she had had taken this year proved that the river once again meandered to the east, taking land from her.

"Madame Chrétien, Monsieur Corbé," Solomon said. "The river has flowed through this valley since the Pleistocene, and over the centuries—nay, millennia!—its course has, on average, barely changed. It was there before Luther and Calvin, yes, even before Jesus Christ. It was there even before the patriarch Abraham. And yet you insist—"

"The photographs prove it," said Adèle. "And they were taken from above, from an airplane."

"Say what you like, maître," was Pierre's reply. "The Chrétiens have profited more than we have. For centuries."

"If that's how you both feel," Eduard said, "then I'm prepared to offer you a solution. Do you want to hear it?"

Pierre and Adèle looked at each other for the first time. Neither showed their hand; what each saw, they already knew. It reminded Pierre of the looks that, as a prisoner of war, he'd exchanged with the guards. It was, in effect, nothing personal.

"I do," said Adèle, at once painfully aware of her inopportune choice of words.

"I'm listening," said Pierre.

Eduard opened a drawer and took out a thin, old-fashioned portfolio fastened with slender ribbons. "May I begin with a personal remark?" he asked, and then continued without waiting for an answer. "I drew this up thirty years ago. Shortly after the Great War, when we all hoped we would be spared anything like it again forever. That, as we know, was not to be. Now we are recovering from a new world war, one that has wounded France profoundly. No one knows this better than you do, madame. Even back then, as a young man, I thought, Surely it must be possible to resolve a private conflict—all things considered, an irrational and unnecessary one—such as yours. Without bloodshed, without animosity, without loss of face, without anyone feeling shortchanged. And I can still present this solution to you, if you wish."

There was a long silence.

"I do," Pierre declared at last, with a wry smile.

"I'm listening," said Adèle.

"You exchange your land," Solomon said.

Everything would stay as it was, except that the western half of the valley would from then on belong to Chrétien, and the eastern half to Corbé. That way no one would henceforth ever have cause to protest the vicissitudes of nature.

Solomon had spoken, and now he waited.

Perhaps coveting the land across the river weighed heavier than relinquishing what they had possessed all their lives, and both Pierre and Adèle were tired of the struggle, the lawsuits, the feuding.

But something else might also have played a role: their common memory of a childhood dream in which they jumped back and forth over the creek, and for a brief moment there was no boundary at all.

They looked at each other. It was not a smile—Adèle never smiled—but something seemed to change, ever so slightly, around the corners of her mouth. Perhaps it was the way the light fell.

Pierre shrugged. "But I'm not paying any solicitor fees."

"That won't be necessary. Madame Chrétien, Monsieur Corbé, I want to bring this protracted case, with which my father and my grandfather wrestled in vain, to a satisfactory close once and for all before I retire. It is, if you will, a personal mission. I shall not levy any fees."

They signed the contract.

His tractor was stuck, sunk to above its axles in the mire in the bend of the river. I'll never learn, Pierre thought, I shouldn't have brought this thing so far down. He stubbornly attempted to extricate himself, but now the tractor would not even start. He had driven off, fully confident that the new machine would be able to stand up to anything. Apparently it could not. Modernity manifested itself in the gasping, ever-weakening gurgle of the exhausted starter motor. It couldn't be an empty fuel tank—he had topped it up from the rusty jerrycan he'd brought along as a reserve. The machine had been given everything it needed, and still it refused to budge. He would have to fetch his horses from the stable to pull the tractor out of the mud.

He did not look forward to going home on foot. That prosthetic leg made it difficult to walk. This was why he brought his hunting rifle with him each workday, as well as the canvas pouch he had used ever since the Great War to carry his bread, sausage, and wine, and ascended the stony hillock in the meadow, where the chapel of Saint Godeberta had once stood, to take his midday break.

It was still strange to survey, from this side of the river, the land that used to be his. He knew every square meter of it, every bush and every branch, just as by now he knew every bush and branch on this side. At times it looked something like the Promised Land, even though he had willingly given it up for what he now possessed. That land swap hadn't made much difference after all; the meadows and woods on this side were just the same. In that respect, he couldn't fault Maître Solomon. And now he understood that the river, seen from this perspective, did not disadvantage either party. This was no longer an issue, ever since Solomon had emigrated to the United States to enjoy his golden years in Florida. He could certainly afford it. Rumor had it that the sale of the villa in Lorient alone had brought in more than half a million francs.

But no, it hadn't gotten any better. He snapped open his pocketknife and cut thin slices of sausage on his thigh. His sheep, which had gathered around him as they grazed, looked on stupidly.

Three Mirages in formation screamed over the valley, and Pierre waited indifferently for the dull boom that would follow when they broke the sound barrier. As long as his tractor did not work, he had little respect for modern technology.

That Corentin Berthou, recently released from jail, had last week denied him the hunting spoils that were rightfully his—the doe he had shot on his land had died on the opposite bank, just one step from the water—was a new declaration of war.

Even though the other side was now another, nothing had changed.

He ruefully observed the hunting parties on the far bank, the way an exiled monarch is forced to watch his former subjects slaughtered. Berthou organized drive hunts. He and his guests were delivered by limousine to the end of the paved road that Corbé himself had built. Their salvo brought down a hundred partridges in a single morning. Wild boars, hares, and lapwings—even the livestock, it seemed—now took cover on his side of the valley.

Pierre was determined, more than ever, to defend his property rights. If anyone, no matter who, dared set foot on what was now and forever his land, he would shoot. This was no idle threat. He would shoot, even if it were Adèle's daughter.

After half an hour, he began to be troubled by the hornets swarming around him. He massaged his stump and refastened the prosthesis. He would give the tractor one last try but did not hold out much hope. That thing was stupider than an animal. Stupider than his dog Babouche, who was now chained up back at the farmhouse, because he could no longer take him along to the valley.

They made better false limbs these days, folks said, but Pierre had decided to make do with this one. The stiff leather cup that fit perfectly around the stump of his lower leg, the steel pipe that had in fact become a bit too long now that he himself had gotten shorter, the hinged block that served as a foot; he had grown accustomed to it. The prosthesis was the price for concealing his transgression, and he paid his debts, down to the last centime and the last minute. I will pay my vows before those who fear Him. No one had ever found out that he had lost his leg in Berthou's fox trap. And they never would. His lips were sealed. He would take this peg leg with him to the grave, even though he reckoned that prostheses did not count at the Resurrection come Judgment Day. Who cares, he thought. So I'll stand before God on one leg. He's seen stranger things.

The shoe on the artificial foot had long been separated from its partner. It was cracked, torn, unoiled, and ancient, nearly fused to the metal staff of the prosthesis. On his good foot he wore something better. Under his bedstead were four or five pristine, never worn right shoes.

He placed his hands on the warm stones to the left and the right, to hoist himself up, and then he saw her.

She wore a dark-red summer dress with flecks or polka dots of a yet darker tint, and she walked along the riverbank.

A strange girl, but that did not absolve her of the guilt of being the progeny of Berthou.

She appeared to be picking flowers; at any rate, she held a few in her hand, but she shuffled along with a drooping head and a dragging gait. Pierre thought she looked terribly lonely, and not entirely normal, and he took a certain amount of pleasure in this. Life spared no one, including the wealthy, neither him nor Adèle Chrétien.

He wiped his fingers on his handkerchief and picked up his shotgun. He would shoot. He would first warn her, but then shoot if she took even one step onto his land.

The girl moved further along the creek, stooping and plucking now and then, as if picking up something she had dropped. She must have seen him by now, sitting atop the tumulus, his silhouette sharp against the blue sky.

She stayed on her own side. Pierre felt in the pocket of his corduroy coat, hesitated, and took out the telescopic sight. This was as good a time as any to try it out. It was a German brand, and he had bought it secondhand. From his other pocket he took out his reading glasses, whose frame, which he had patched together with adhesive tape, was so wobbly that it hung lopsidedly on his nose when he tried to attach the sight to the rifle. It had gone easier at home, at the kitchen table. When the sight was finally fastened and he looked up, the girl was still there, crouching to pull a flower from the grass.

He raised his gun and pressed his right eye against the eyepiece. He didn't see anything. Distance needs adjusting, he thought. He twisted the black knob on the right side of the scope. At first everything became even blurrier, but then the world came into view. A tiny portion of the world. Her pale, skinny legs in low rubber boots, in which she waded into the water. Don't do it, he thought. It was wondrous: He looked through a cross, the symbol of redemption, and what was beyond it he could kill by simply pulling the trigger.

He tried aiming slightly higher while turning the knob: the red fabric of her dress flashed past, he saw all the dark spots on it, and then he saw her face. She was looking at him.

What a homely girl. She'd obviously inherited the worst genes of the Berthous and the Chrétiens combined. Big nose, red hair. The sliver of creation contained in the circle of his telescopic sight was far from the prettiest.

The crosshairs descended back down to her boots, which now stood on a pair of stones in the middle of the river.

The Mirages returned, as if to smash the sound barrier from the other side, and the valley was flattened under the roar of the jet engines.

"Halt!" he shouted. "One more step and I'll shoot!"

The cross flew upward, and he bent his index finger.

The girl clamped her hands over her ears and stuck out her tongue. The two handfuls of wildflowers made it look as though she were crowning herself, a heathen creature that stood there, mocking him.

The anticipated sonic boom did not happen. Instead, the roar died out, and the jet fighters banked northward, heading back to the base in Cambrai.

Pierre stood up and lowered his shotgun.

“Go away!” he shouted, gesticulating wildly. His voice sounded thin and irrelevant in the vast landscape, which, like him, still seemed deafened by the ferocity of the Mirages overhead. “Be off!”

She stayed put on the stones in the middle of the river and shouted something he did not understand. Then she turned and went away. Once she reached the shore, she threw down the flowers she'd plucked, and ran off.

The next day Pierre came back with two horses and pulled the tractor out of the muck. He noticed that something had changed, but couldn't put his finger on it. Something about the contour of the meadow near the tumulus. Land didn't change, he knew that, but still it looked different than the day before. His suspicions piqued, he wondered if Solomon had cheated him after all, or whether there was something else not quite right about the land that was now his. He brought the horses to a halt and went to investigate. He could have sworn that the shadow cast by the low-lying sun fell differently over the grassland than before. A bramble bush that had basked in sunlight at this time yesterday was now in the dark. That was impossible. Stopping halfway up the hillock, Pierre looked around warily. Horses, chain, tractor, hitch, and cart still stood like a long, stationary frieze down on the bank of the glistening river. Nor did the woods or the clouds look particularly unusual. Everything seemed the same, but something was different, although he didn't yet know what.

Suddenly he sank, both legs at once, into the ground. The land he mistrusted was swallowing him. He braced himself with both arms, and subsided no further. He waited for the pain, like when he had stepped into the fox trap, but it did not come. He was up to his hips in the ground; besides this, there was nothing amiss. He bent his arms and tried to pull himself out, his elbows cocked like the handles of a corkscrew, but underneath him the earth gave way, and he felt his foot and prosthesis dangle in thin air. Pierre remained still for a while, for sometimes that was the best thing. Thinking it through might help, he thought, but where to start? He was alone in the vale aside from the yoked horses, and from them he couldn't expect any help.

While his pocket watch in the grass counted the minutes, he noticed other things that were different. The river behind the cart looked narrower than some twenty meters further up, in front of the drooping heads of his horses. And now that he focused on the sounds of the world, he heard, in addition to the wind and the crows, another sound coming from the depths below him: running water. He could even smell it, a muddy, musty odor rising up around his torso.

Pierre leaned forward, pressed his upper body into the turf and groped for sturdy clumps of grass. Slowly, ever so slowly, no need to hurry, he pulled himself out of the hole. Stalks, weeds, goat droppings, and a ladybug passed his wide-open eyes. Just as he carefully slid his hips onto the crumbling edge, the ground gave way underneath him, like a mattress on a sagging bed. He lay stock-still, two sturdily rooted thistles clamped in his fists, and waited for a while, until nothing more happened, before crawling further and grabbing hold of a boulder, where he could sit.

The shoe that he had worn on his artificial foot was gone; he hobbled back to his horses, giving the treacherous ground a wide berth. The horses looked up lazily, as though they regretted he hadn't stayed away for longer.

The following edition of *l'Ouest-Éclair* carried, in addition to news of the war in Indochina and the resignation of Prime Minister Mendès France, a brief regional item:

> *The long-running dispute between the Chrétien and Corbé families, frequently reported by this journal for the past hundred years, has apparently taken a new and unexpected twist. The uncommon exchange of their properties in the Issou valley (*sous-préfecture de Pontivy*) in 1953, intended to put an end to the dispute, now seems to have benefited one of the parties in an unforeseen manner. On the eastern bank of the river, since time immemorial in the possession of the Chrétien family but now the property of the unmarried M. Pierre Corbé, a Merovingian holy site is said to have been discovered, which according to archaeologists dates from the seventh century and was probably dedicated to*

Saint Godeberta. It likely contains relics and artifacts of inestimable value that would make the owner of the property a wealthy man. The valley is closed to visitors for the duration of the excavations. M. Berthou, the husband of the original owner, Adèle Chrétien, has indicated he shall contest M. Corbé's ownership rights and the subsequent revenues in the highest courts of the land. Mme. Chrétien and M. Corbé were unavailable for comment, as was Maître Solomon, the former solicitor from Lorient and the initiator of the land exchange, who currently resides in faraway America and is said to enjoy a position of stature in the well-to-do Jewish community of Boca Raton in Florida. This writer shall continue to keep our readers, who undoubtedly follow this extraordinary affair with as much interest as himself, abreast of all new developments.

Corentin flung her onto the bed and laid into her with his fists.

Adèle had never been able to fend off her husband's violent attacks. If he had been drinking, he hit her; it had been like this since their wedding night. Brute force was the only thing in which Corentin Berthou was her superior. She pitied him, as the blood gushed from her nose. She was ashamed of him, now that he tore open his shirt, exposing his hairless, suety chest, and slowly pulled his belt from his trousers. He was nothing, he was a lost soul, and she had to live with it.

"Think of the child," was all she said.

"Child?" he said, winding the belt around his fist. "Don't pretend you care about her. That mutt should never have been born."

There had been that one night when she stood over him with a knife in her hand. She didn't do it. Justice and dignity were still her domain. She, a mother, would rather be humiliated and beaten like a whore than give him a taste of his own medicine, no matter how much he debased himself.

He pushed her face into the pillow and pulled up her nightdress.

"Jew whore," he said. "You threw away our land behind my back while I was in prison. Did you suck his circumcised cock, heh? I could have been rich! A millionaire! And now that bum Corbé will make off with the loot. Goddamned Catholic loot, on top of it." He beat her mercilessly on her back and her thighs. "A Christian shrine!"

"Corentin, stop! The child . . ."

"The child—bullshit! Corentin—bullshit! I'll teach you, bitch!" He beat her left and right, lost his balance, and caught himself on the bedpost.

Adèle turned and tried to sit up. "You're drunk, man! Stop it. Stop it!"

He punched her squarely in the face. This was the first time he struck her with his closed fist; normally he hit her with his open hand. He sucked on his knuckles, surprised, and wiped them on his trousers, grinned, and hit her again with an uppercut worthy of Marcel Cerdan.

"Not too drunk to show you who's boss . . ."

She fell back on the pillow and frantically reached for her nose. It felt broken.

He picked up his beer bottle, saw that it was empty, started to cry, and whipped her with the belt. "Down! *Couche-toi!* Down!" he screamed, and Adèle plugged her ears, as if doing so might prevent her daughter from hearing.

Marie-France lay stock-still under the duvet, her dolls and teddy bear clasped in her arms, a corner of the pillowcase in her mouth. Usually this was enough to fall asleep, even though she didn't much like sleep because then she couldn't keep her ear to the ground and couldn't think, and felt somehow like she was abandoning herself. But tonight she closed her eyes as tight as she could and pretended she was asleep, so as not to have to hear what was happening in her parents' bedroom.

She knew why no one loved her. The true, actual, secret reason was that she had come into this world to do something marvelous and extraordinary, and until she had done that, no one would ever love her. Those were the special rules that applied only to her. That's also why she wasn't as cute as the other children. But she was a chosen one, so it would all work out in the end.

"Bullshit," Papa had shouted, and Mama had only whimpered. Maybe even Mama wasn't convinced deep in her heart that she should have been born.

The farmer across the valley, that Huguenot who had made off with their treasure, was a coward. She had provoked him earlier that day, just to test him. She didn't feel sorry for him, even though he was crippled. And he had pointed a rifle at her, which at least showed he took her seriously. She had fussed around with some flowers, but that was just for show. He only yelled, just like Papa, go away and suchlike, but he didn't shoot, not even above her head. But he did have a treasure that wasn't his at all. He sat on that hill with his rifle, and that hill wasn't even his. That land had always been theirs, treasure and all.

She put the dolls and the teddy bear in the drawer of her nightstand. It was time for them to go, just like the lambs that went to slaughter every year.

When Marie-France lay back, her arms crossed over her chest underneath the duvet, she had a revelation, the best one she'd ever had.

She would heroically steal back their rightful property, not even for herself, but for her parents, and everyone would be in awe of her. And when she came home with the treasure, she would pretend the Holy Mother of God had guided her there; and she would say: "The Holy Mother of God told me to do this, so that all fathers and mothers would know they have to love unto little girls, the way I love them," or some such thing.

And then her father would lift her up and exclaim: "This is truly my daughter!" And Pierre Corbé would have to swim, gnashing his teeth, in a pool of burning phosphorus, but even for him it would turn out well in the end because purgatory was only temporary. And her mother would sigh and say, "Oh my child, I have always loved you dearly, more than you will ever know."

In fact, she would be just like Joan of Arc, who eventually married the king of France.

Now that the idea had taken root, she couldn't sleep a wink.

She heard slamming doors, and in between slams she could hear her mother weep.

A car engine started, which always meant that Papa had left.

Tomorrow, she thought, I'll do it.

Tomorrow everything will be fine.

Berthou pressed the gas pedal to the floor and sped through the first curve, the headlights skimmed the deathly pale foliage of the plane trees, and a salvo of stones and gravel sprayed out from under the rear tires. He sat hunched over, his hands clamped to the steering wheel. He had saliva on his chin, and he swatted the rearview mirror angrily so as not to have to see himself. He downshifted to achieve maximum acceleration, before having to brake again at the end of the drive. He preferred not to have to brake at all, but it was a necessary evil if you wanted to keep control of the vehicle. But he did so as savagely as possible, using the foot and hand brakes simultaneously, a trick he could execute perfectly, and sent the car hurtling through the curve. He opened the throttle again on the straight stretch through the woods and hugged the snaking white line in the middle of the asphalt. Bitch . . . traitors . . . not the master of one's own home . . . Jewish plutocrats . . . coerced into marrying under his station by his father . . . a peasant woman who couldn't give him a son, only a hideous mutt, a caricature of himself. He needed to piss, and slammed on the brakes when the wall of the British war cemetery loomed ahead.

He left the engine running and the headlights on, the car parked diagonally on the shoulder; let everybody see, for all he cared. His trousers sagged as he pushed open the wrought-iron gate, for he'd left his belt in the bedroom. He took the second path to the right, his favorite place to urinate, where the gravestones did not display a cross but the Star of David and oriental symbols. He pissed against a stone belonging to one Balbur Singh, killed in action in 1918, and thought: Good thing no one sees me crying. No sir, I'll not give them the pleasure. He returned to his car and tried to open the trunk, hoping there might be a bottle with a dreg of eau-de-vie left, but it was locked, and to open it he first had to turn off the ignition.

Imbeciles, those Renault makers. American cars had a handle so you could open the trunk from the inside. He hated nothing, except his wife and himself, more than Renault. Once the trunk was open, he saw there was no bottle. He returned to the graveyard and drank from the garden hose. Midnight mist hung motionlessly between the woods on either side of the road. The illuminated hands of the dashboard clock showed that it was two o'clock.

He was desperate for alcohol but did not want to go back home, not at any price. The Relais des Routiers at the bridge, then. It would be closed, of course, but the *patron* owed him a favor, so he could rouse him from bed if necessary. Maybe there were customers still drinking and playing cards behind the closed shutters, as was often the case.

Berthou took the last dark curves with more luck than skill, parked inconspicuously behind the trucks at the side of the road, and got out. The inn was dark—even the neon sign had been turned off. It was quiet. The four tall lamps on the concrete bridge offered the only light between the dark hillsides. He wouldn't think twice about pounding on the door, hollering and shaking up the entire joint, but first he leaned over the iron railing, which was orange but looked black in the light of the sodium lamps. The river flowed below him, black and narrow. What a godforsaken hellhole he had got himself into.

Looking over his shoulder, he noticed that the front truck was loaded with oil drums. It was parked on the shoulder, and the bank inclined sharply.

Berthou retraced his steps and took a closer look. Came from Brest, destination Le Mans. Hundreds of twenty-four-gallon drums, stacked three high. Tens of thousands of liters of refined, highly flammable fuel oil. Truck's cabin the height of the railing. Nothing but the steep embankment between the cargo bed and river. He could send a river of fire downstream, which would send that whole cursed treasure of Corbé's up in flames. He would finish off that damn valley of Adèle's once and for all. They had all underestimated him.

A stinking layer of oil flowed through the valley, an opalescent ribbon winding between the dark hillsides. The Relais des Routiers stood at the foot of the bridge, just as dead and dumb as always. Think clearly now, Berthou said to himself. How long does oil burn? No time for mistakes. I won't light it just yet. How fast does this blasted river flow? He lit his last cigarette, threw the empty pack into the water, and followed it with his eyes. Say about three kilometers per hour. How far from here to the tumulus? He'd need the Michelin map for that. He would drive along the riverbank on the paved road Corbé, the dolt, had put in himself, and there he would set the carpet of oil on fire.

He started his engine as quietly as possible, obediently switched on his turn signal, and drove west.

Pierre lay in bed. He could hardly believe his luck.

He had become a wealthy man overnight. His finder's fee, as the owner of the land, could be hundreds of thousands, perhaps even a million francs. Praise the Lord, now and forever. God gives to his beloved in their sleep. Our children and grandchildren shall tell of Your goodness. If there were relics in the crypt, then they might even make it into the Louvre.

How could any man sleep if his fate took such an extraordinary turn? He felt for the braided electrical cord of his nightstand lamp and found the switch. Three a.m. Just a few more hours and then it would be light enough to go out and gaze upon the site of his miraculous discovery.

He would be able to buy an electric milking machine, like the one he'd seen at the agricultural fair in Rennes. And the Lord gave Job fourteen thousand sheep and a thousand yoke of oxen, each and every brow bedecked with gilded garlands.

Pierre could not stay in bed; he was overjoyed beyond measure.

He got up and made coffee.

The Lord's ways are mysterious, but righteous. He would not have seven sons and three daughters, but a few large barns, anyway, and maybe a new house.

It was dawn, with a little fantasy. He put on his coat and brought food out to the dog, who would stay in its kennel. Babouche eyed him with mistrust and reproach at being left behind.

"Soon everything will be different, Babouche," Pierre said. "You'll see."

The Lord God is my strength, he will make my feet like the deer's, and shall make me walk upon the heights. Pierre hobbled excitedly along the right bank of the river, anxious to revisit the corrugated iron roof and the festive rectangle of barbed wire that protected his treasure from the livestock. As a Protestant he scorned the veneration of saints, but even so, Godeberta, if she truly did repose on his land, deserved better than a field strewn with goat dung.

Suddenly something off in the distance glimmered at him. Something that had not been there before. And the next moment a small moving figure appeared. Things were happening in a place where nothing at all should happen until the archaeologists returned. He was still too far away to see what it was, and picked up his limping pace.

It was the Chrétien girl, and she was stealing part of his treasure. He did not call out, for he wanted to get a little closer first; but she saw him and stood up, a golden chest cradled in her arms, and started running toward the river.

"Stay right there, you!" Pierre shouted, and also broke into a run, something he had not attempted since the amputation.

She glanced over her shoulder and was clever enough not to wade into the river directly, but to give herself a head start; he saw the soles of her sandals and her dancing braids.

Pierre followed, hobbling determinedly, but his prosthesis could not keep up with his good leg.

Fortunately her judgment eventually abandoned her, and she leapt into the river, just at the spot where the water was at its deepest and split around a few large boulders. She disappeared underwater—all that was visible was a tiny pair of hands holding up the chest. It was no bigger than a shoebox. He waded into the river, lost his balance on the slippery rocks, fell to his knees, stood back up, dripping, and extended his arms.

"Give it here, you little guttersnipe!"

She surfaced as a hideous fish, with wide-open eyes, still clasping the chest, which had relief-ornamented edges and a small opaque window in the middle.

"No!" she shrieked. "It belongs to my papa!"

"I'll teach you," Pierre said, grabbing hold of her wrist. "Let go, or I'll drown you like a cat!"

She shrieked again, as loudly as she could, and hurled the casket into the river, whereupon it was carried off and then sank. Pierre held the body of the little girl underwater between his legs as he tried to locate it.

And then there was an unearthly, roaring whoosh. Pierre looked up and saw, in the distance, a wave of flames barreling toward them. The livestock on both riverbanks ran up the hillsides, birds flapped away, and an enormous column of black smoke sped down the valley, its upper layers as powerful as God's clenched fury, the lower part a funnel that followed the meanders of the river. The Day of Judgment had come. Behold, the Lord comes with fire, and his chariots are like a whirlwind. The heat punched him in the face. It was all over. A raging wall of flames rushed at him. He turned and saw the small golden shrine sparkle from under the surface.

She knew without looking in the mirror that her nose was broken. She would lie to the doctor that a cow's horn had unwittingly hit her in the face, just as in the past she had explained away broken fingers and burn wounds as household mishaps.

She washed her face with cold water, dried it off, and examined it in the mirror. More than the swollen, crooked nose, she was shocked by her thin, cheerless mouth and the stony eyes. Beauty, gone forever. She hung the wet towel on the hook next to the small bathroom window and looked outside.

It was the rosy-fingered dawn, the only thing by Homer she remembered, but the slice of the eastern sky framed by the thick window sash was dominated by an immense column of black smoke.

She could not imagine what kind of fire that might be in the remote valley.

Adèle ran to the bedroom and quickly dressed; Berthou was gone, she would have to go look herself. She flung open the door to Marie-France's bedroom.

Pierre waded unsteadily downstream toward the chest, his arms spread wide to keep his balance.

There it was, a meter deep, pushed up against the curve of a rock by the current, curiously wavering, as if debating which side of the obstacle to glide off. He bent over and thrust his arms into the water.

The child screamed, the wall of fire had reached them, the black smoke towering above them like an enormous anvil. The vanguard of flames surrounded her. She threw her skinny arms in the air.

Pierre had the casket in his hands. He did not do what he wanted to do, but rather as he had been trained on the front. He dared not throw the shrine onto the bank, as though he was holding an unfamiliar and hazardous explosive, but rather let go of it and wrestled his way upstream, straight at the fire.

The girl floated toward him like a burning doll.

"Hush now," he heard himself absurdly call out.

The flames now engulfed him, and he felt his beard, skin, and hair ripped away for good. Our God is a consuming fire. He caught her in his arms and ducked underwater with her.

Underwater was better, much better, only there was no air. She floundered and thrashed, but he held her tight. She wouldn't drown in just twenty seconds. He expected to hear something, God's raging fury, but he heard nothing unnatural, so he opened his eyes and looked. There was an intense light above him, and he thought, This is the last thing I'll ever see. He had bungled everything, he had failed, he had no right to any happiness whatsoever. But the Lord wanted him, not this child. He held his breath, grabbed hold of heavy stones in order to stay submerged, and pushed her head down. It may be you shall be hid in the day of the Lord's wrath.

Then it was over, and he had to either breathe or die. He took the limp body in his arms and surfaced.

Foul muck oozed around them. The first thing he saw float by was a large red drum with the word "TOTAL" on it. Smoke trailed behind the receding fire like black voile. The oil fumes made him gag. The Lord works in mysterious ways.

He sought a foothold on the stony bottom. Oil vapors burned his eyes. The world looked round, as though viewed through a distorting lens.

A woman in a brown shawl flapping around her shoulders came running along the opposite bank.

She stopped unexpectedly, right in front of him, her arms outstretched and hands open, with a curiously disfigured face.

Of course, the child must be with her mother, and then he could go home.

He stood up, the child in his arms, and waded to the Chrétiens' side, which had been his and his forefathers' for so very long, to do what he had to do, what anyone else would do.

He felt nothing except the knowledge that he had not abandoned God.

There were traces of oil on his burned head. Wisps of smoke whirled around him while he rose up out of the water, right before Adèle's eyes, cradling her child. The little arms and legs hung like immobile bell-clappers.

He climbed onto the riverbank, tottering every other step, because his prosthesis no longer had a shoe.

"Here," he said, and laid the child against Adèle's breast. "I have to go home now."

Adèle ran with her child along the western bank, while Pierre stumbled off in the opposite direction. The column of smoke, less imposing than it had been, disappeared into the distance.

"Maman, Maman," Marie-France whimpered. The half of her face that was visible among the folds of the brown shawl was contorted in fear. "There was nothing I could do. I already had the treasure, but then he came, and then the fire . . ."

"My sweetheart, my brave child," she whispered. "You have saved us all."

I can sleep in her bed tonight, Marie-France thought to herself, and then it will all have been worth the trouble.

Eduard Solomon treated himself to a flight on the Concorde for his last trip to Brittany. He spoiled himself these days: he was eighty-six years old and had prostate cancer. During the descent into Paris, he tried to make out the coastline and smiled as he thought of Asterix and Obelix and their "small village in Gaul, which stubbornly holds out against the invaders." But under the thick white cloud cover, he saw only the tip of Normandy, and then they landed at Charles de Gaulle.

He wondered how the Chrétiens and the Corbés had fared since all the fuss about the discovery of that treasure. Like so many Americans, he was addicted to television series and was as curious about these two families' narrative as when he had missed several episodes of *Dallas* while on a sailing trip.

He had made an open-ended reservation for a suite at L'Ermitage in La Baule.

With the first-class carriage to himself, he set his feet on a newspaper on the seat across from him. The latest Saul Bellow novel, still in its cellophane wrapping, sat on his lap. He didn't feel much like reading, certainly not something American. He watched the landscape glide past and wondered if he would ever see it glide past in the opposite direction. Maybe not. Perhaps, like his literary hero, Nabokov in Montreux, he would spend his last days in a grand hotel.

When the train pulled into Chartres a solitary female traveler entered his compartment, and Solomon politely removed his feet from the seat, despite her smiling assurance that it wasn't necessary. He valued old-fashioned courtesy, especially now that he was back in Europe.

The newspaper under his feet turned out to be *l'Ouest-Éclair*, the regional paper.

He skipped the first section, having already perused the international journals during the flight. He wanted the local news and remembered where to find it. He even looked forward to reading the advertisements, if only to see whether the delicatessen in Lorient still advertised its celebrated saucisson.

The article that caught his eye began with the headline: *Chapel of Saint Godeberta Dedicated.*

> *A momentous day for Catholic Brittany: Today, Monseigneur Gouyon, archbishop of Rennes, dedicated the chapel of Saint Godeberta, located in the remote Issou valley. At the spot where the property's owner, M. Corbé—himself, it should be noted, a practicing Protestant—discovered the crypt and the golden shrine containing the bones of this little-known seventh-century martyr, a striking octagonal edifice has been constructed, designed by the architecture firm Bervets & Sons in Nantes. The building was financed entirely from private means, in particular by Mme. Adèle Berthou (née Chrétien), the widow of the controversial Corentin Berthou, who, shortly after the sensational archaeological discovery, was tragically killed in an automobile accident.*
>
> *The remarkable edifice will in future certainly attract the attention of the rare hiker taking in the charming but inaccessible vale of the Issou, although many readers will share the opinion of your editor that our landscape has not been enhanced by a*

creation on par with, for instance, Le Corbusier's Notre-Dame-du-Haut . . .

I'll never understand these people, Solomon thought to himself. The story was accompanied by a grainy black-and-white photograph. He took out his magnifying glass.

The caption read: *Proudly reunited: the donor, Mme. Adèle Berthou, her daughter Mlle. Marie-France, law graduate of the Sorbonne, and the tolerant landowner, M. Pierre Corbé.*

Adèle looked distinguished, in a buttoned-up overcoat and a hat sporting what appeared to be lapwing feathers. Pierre looked down and had a cropped gray beard. He was small—much smaller than Adèle, who gazed resolutely into the lens, and her daughter, who stood in between them. He wore a bowler hat and looked remarkably well kempt. He leaned, his ankles crossed, on a walking stick that he had planted diagonally in the grass. He looked a bit like General Lee in his final days. Marie-France smiled gaily, despite the solemnity of the occasion: an emancipated young woman in a plaid miniskirt. Her curly hair, even in the black-and-white photo, seemed to light up under her beret.

ABOUT THE AUTHOR

Photo © 2015 Bob Bronshoff

Martin Michael Driessen is a Dutch opera and theater director, translator, and writer. He made his debut in 1999 with the novel *Gars*, followed by *Vader van God* (*Father of God*, 2012) and *Een ware held* (*A True Hero*, 2013), both of which were broadly reviewed and nominated for literary prizes. In 2015 his novel *Lizzie*, written with the highly acclaimed and prize-nominated poet Liesbeth Lagemaat, was published under the pseudonym Eva Wanjek. *Rivieren* (*Rivers*) was awarded the prestigious ECI Literature Prize (formerly the AKO) in 2016. His latest novel, *De pelikaan* (*The Pelican*), was published in 2017. His work has been translated into English, Italian, German, and Hungarian.

ABOUT THE TRANSLATOR

Photo © 2015 Michele Hutchison

Jonathan Reeder, a native of upstate New York and longtime resident of Amsterdam, enjoys a dual career as a literary translator and performing musician. Along with his work as a professional bassoonist, he translates opera libretti and essays on classical music as well as contemporary Dutch fiction and poetry. His first two translated novels—*The Cocaine Salesman* by Conny Braam and *Bonita Avenue* by Peter Buwalda—were longlisted for the International IMPAC Dublin Literary Award, and Bram Dehouck's comic thriller *A Sleepless Summer* (winner of the 2012 Golden Noose) was selected by the Sunday Times Crime Club as a "December pick." Additional English translations include novels and short stories by Mano Bouzamour, Christine Otten, Hanna Bervoets, and A.F.Th. van der Heijden.